Praise for *Agent D...*

Mecha-Mo...

"Don't quote me in the front of your book."

-My Uncle

"I knew Grant when he couldn't even write a single sentence. Now, he can write lots of sentences in a row."

-My Aunt

"Fiction is making stuff up, which is basically lying. This book is proof that Grant is talented at lying."

-My Friends

"Mr. Goodman is the best author ever."

-Actual Comment From a Former Student

AGENT DARCY & NINJA STEVE

1. TIGER TROUBLE

2. ROBOT RUMBLE

3. MECHA-MOLE MAYHEM

4. ????????????????????

5. ????????????????????

Agent Darcy

&

Ninja Steve:
Mecha-Mole Mayhem

By Grant Goodman

To Dr. Siriboe!

Thank you for setting up
an amazing interview ᴗ

Grant Good

To Dr. Siriboe!
Thank you for setting up oo
an amazing interview ♡

[signature]

ISBN-13: 978-1977751324

ISBN-10: 1977751326

Edition 1.3

Disclaimer: The following story is a work of fiction. Regarding the events in this book, any similarity to any person, living, dead, or undead is merely coincidental.

For Heather

STEVE

"I never should have gone to Botsylvania," said Steve, as he lay on his thin, roll-out mattress in his prison cell.

He had said the same thing every morning since he had been put in jail, twenty days ago. He had a feeling that he'd be saying it every day for the remaining forty days of his imprisonment.

Every time he said it, he thought back to the judge putting a ridiculous white wig over his ninja hood, banging a nunchaku on the desk, and proclaiming, "Sixty days of prison for Ninja Steve."

It was lonely here, mostly because he was the only ninja who was in the juvenile prison. Samurai Sam faced no penalty because he wasn't involved in using a fart bomb on the police, directly defying President Ninja's orders, or using a technique before he was thirteen.

Ninjastoria didn't have a crime problem, so the jail for juveniles only had three cells and the adult prison building down the road only had five. Nora had been sent to the adult prison.

He wasn't totally lonely, though, as his parents stopped by every day to give him the school work he was missing. Steve actually found that it was easy to get all of his homework done when he had fewer distractions. For the first time in his life, he had an A in every class.

In his cell, wearing the red uniform that all jailed ninjas had to wear, Steve did a hundred jumping jacks to warm up, then knocked out a few rounds of push-ups, burpees, and jump-squats.

By then, he had worked up a good sweat.

He started some stretches, only to be interrupted by the voice from the ceiling speaker.

"WE ARE UNDER ATTACK! THE MECHA-MOLES HAVE APPEARED IN NINJASTORIA! DON'T PANIC! THERE IS NO NEED TO PANIC! AHHHHHHHH!"

Steve was close to panicking when he remembered the first chapter of the book that Sensei Raheem had given to him to read in prison: *Sensei Raheem's Guide to Supreme Ninja Skills (and Tomato Gardening)*. Steve had been reading a chapter a day...and had been learning good stuff from it, to his surprise. The first chapter had been all about fear. The way it crept into your mind, the way it unraveled your strength, the way it could twist your life into a miserable little shadow. Then, Sensei Raheem taught you how to fight it.

"Admit that you feel fear," Ninja Steve told himself. "Then, face it."

He heard the sounds of battle. The shouts of ninjas, the clang of metal striking metal, the thumps of heavy footsteps. Steve backed himself into a corner and then jumped up onto the ceiling. The mecha-moles were fond of the ground, so Steve reasoned that they might come up through the floor.

The noises got louder and louder. The fight had reached his hallway.

Steve's cell gate was torn off of its hinges. A pack of five scout mecha-moles came surging through on all fours. Their bodies were green like avocados and their pointy snouts all pointed at Ninja Steve. The metal claws that coated their real claws were extra bright, and even though the moles were only about three feet tall when they chose to stand on their hind legs, their bodies were wide and heavy.

There was no sign of anyone coming to help him.

"You can do this," Steve told himself. "You've fought them before."

That time, however, he had been with Sensei Raheem. When you were with Sensei Raheem, there was no way you were going to lose. The book, however, specifically said that you *didn't* need Sensei Raheem in order to win, but that it *was* tremendously helpful to have him there.

Steve swooped down from the ceiling like a hawk-squirrel and thrust a kick into a mecha-mole's chest. The squat creature went flying.

"Surrender," one of the others barked at Steve.

Steve looked at them. Many against one. More in the hallway. Could he win?

"What do you think, Ninja Steve? Would you like to surrender?"

Steve looked up at the ceiling behind him. Standing there was the man in the gray mask with three red slashes across it.

"I'm not surrendering," Steve said. "Especially if I have to surrender to *you*."

Steve had never trusted him. The first time their paths had crossed, the man had been talking with Toran the Tiger. The time after that, he had flung Nora through the kitchen window of their house.

The man in the mask laughed. "Are you sure?"

"Yeah. I'd rather fight than surrender."

"Good," said the man. "I don't believe I've ever properly introduced myself. My name is Three."

Three jumped off of the ceiling. Steve dipped low, ready to throw an uppercut. But Three leaped *over* Steve, and punched a mecha-mole so hard that it broke through the bars of the prison cell across the hall.

"Let's fight them together, Ninja Steve," Three said.

Steve didn't have time to ask questions. He got ready to kick some mecha-mole butt.

DARCY

Darcy lay on her bedroll, staring at the cream-colored wall. She had the covers pulled up to her chin. The sun would be rising soon and she hadn't slept well.

After Darcy had been kicked out of the Bureau of Sneakery for being part of the Botsylvania battle, Gertie and her husband, Morris, had taken her in, given her a room of her own. The trade was simple: a place to stay in exchange for becoming a serious ninja.

While she lay there in the early morning darkness, she thought about how easily she had been thrown away. How she had been so emotionally empty even after Ninja Steve's parents told her they'd found her a place to live in Ninjastoria, a village where she had more friends than she'd ever had at the bureau.

At sunrise, Darcy's door opened.

"Get up," Gertie said, and the iron in her voice made Darcy jump. Although Gertie was tiny and old and wrinkled, she had incredible posture and poise. "We have work to do, and there won't be any time to feel sorry for yourself."

That morning, Darcy chopped logs with an axe until she was sure that someone had set her limbs on fire. That afternoon, she helped Gertie prepare a garlic-studded rib roast and whipped sweet potatoes with autumn spice butter. And that evening, she began her meditation sessions, where she had to tell herself that the past was done.

Sure enough, it brought her back to life.

Every single day after that started with combat in the training room, even school days.

It was a long, rectangular room in the backyard, attached to the main house by an open-air hallway. The walls, floors, and ceiling were covered in thick, black pads. Gertie and Morris had removable hooks in some parts of the walls so that they could hang up punching bags if they wanted.

Today was not a punching bag day.

Darcy dove a half-second before Gertie's kick would have caught her in the face. She landed facedown on the training room's bamboo floor, flipped over onto her back, and sprang up to her feet before the next strike came in.

Sweat was dripping down into her eyes and there was no time to wipe it away. If she diverted her attention, she'd get hit.

Duck. Roll. Swerve. Bend.

Each strike came in and each time — barely — she managed to evade.

Hop. Shift. Turn.

She let the punch slide past her, grazing her shoulder ever so slightly, and when she thought she had an opening, she threw her punch.

"Too slow," Ninja Gertie said.

She caught Darcy by the wrist, and whirled her in a circle so that Darcy tumbled to the ground.

Darcy gritted her teeth together and pulled herself up. She bowed to Ninja Gertie. The tiny, old woman bowed back.

"You're still hesitating," Gertie said.

"Yes," Darcy said. "However —"

"No excuses," Gertie told her. Despite being the village's oldest ninja, she was as tough as chromega. "The more breath you waste making excuses, the less you have for fighting."

Darcy bowed low. "Yes."

"Wash up, change your uniform, and meet me in the kitchen so I can teach you how to make my famous blue curry stir-fry. The perfect balance of flavor and spice is hard to get right."

Darcy bowed yet again. "Yes."

Ninja Gertie walked away and Darcy did some cool-down stretches before she went back to her room.

It was the exact same room she had shared with Serena when they had arrived on their first mission. Even though Serena wouldn't have been her first choice of roommate, Darcy sometimes found herself wishing that someone from the bureau was there to talk to her.

"That was the past," Darcy told herself. "The past is gone and this is your life now."

Gertie had made her repeat that over and over. At first, it had made Darcy upset, having to constantly confront the reality of her expulsion. Eventually, though, it started to become calming.

After Darcy was done showering and had changed into her casual ninja uniform—she still couldn't tell what made it different from the training ninja uniform—she went upstairs to the kitchen.

Along the way, she wondered how Ninja Steve was doing. Darcy had been at Steve's trial following the Botsylvania incident. When it was all over and Steve had been sentenced to prison time, she had watched President Ninja pick Steve up and literally throw him in jail.

Nora's sentencing had been different. No one was going to throw her anywhere. When Darcy had learned that Nora had actually punched President Ninja in the face, she had assumed that Nora would be in jail for at least ten years. Instead, she got six months in the adult prison. President Ninja had argued that because Nora was already a college graduate, she needed to be tried as an adult.

Neither Steve nor Nora were allowed visitors other than immediate family for the first month, but Darcy planned on going the first day that she could. Until then, she was writing letters to both of them. In her most recent one, she had told them about Gertie's kitchen tips for making fluffier pancakes.

When Darcy reached the kitchen, Gertie threw a black apron across the room and it landed perfectly around Darcy's neck. Gertie had done this pretty much every day and it never ceased to be impressive.

"Marcy, the first step is the same as always: locate and organize all of your ingredients."

Her fake name, which had only been meant to last for a few months while she was an exchange student, was now permanent.

Gertie handed her an index card that contained a list of everything she needed. The handwriting was crisp and neat, as if it had come from a printer.

Darcy was picking up a bottle of cooking oil when Gertie leaped over the table and threw a jump kick. Darcy dodged, but dropped the bottle.

"Not good enough," Gertie said. "Now, get back to work."

Darcy did as she was told.

While they prepped ingredients, Gertie put on one of Ninja Bruce's famous songs. He was a classic ninja rock star, although Darcy had never heard of him. The song was all about a regular ninja trying to get by, making and selling his own shurikens, and how it made him very tired, but it was honest work. Darcy hummed along, because she still didn't know all the words.

"They never taught us cooking at the b…at my old school," Darcy said.

Gertie grinned. "That's simply not fair. Everyone should learn how to cook and how to bake, girls *and* guys."

Darcy started chopping onions and bright blue pow-peppers. She continued humming. The bureau never would have let her do anything like this. Meals were prepared for them so that they could spend more time studying. The only exception had been the café where Matilda worked.

"Marcy, I hear someone walking toward the front door. Please go answer it," Gertie said as she sliced up green beans.

Darcy got to the door as their visitor knocked.

She opened it and found Ninja Steph there. They were both in Sensei Poh-Shen's chemistry class. Steph wore a shiny, black ninja uniform and red tabi boots. She kept her wavy hair in a bun and was always chewing strawberry bubblegum. The two of them had been randomly paired for an upcoming project on how to make rainbow smoke bombs. She and Darcy hadn't exactly gotten along.

"Hi," Darcy said.

"Hey, Marcy," Steph said. "Nice apron."

"Oh, we're making blue curry stir-fry," Darcy said.

"Wow," said Steph, chewing loudly on her gum. "I thought Gertie was supposed to be toughening you up, not teaching you how to open a restaurant. In fact, shouldn't you be practicing standing on the ceiling? That must have been really embarrassing in class yesterday when you couldn't do it."

Darcy frowned. All of the other ninjas had been able to stand on the ceiling since they were toddlers.

Darcy let it go. "What can I help you with?"

Steph blew a bubble and popped it with her teeth, then handed over a scroll tied with a ribbon. Darcy opened it.

"Both of you have been summoned to Sensei Poh-Shen's office at 7:00 PM."

She looked at Steph.

"I'll meet you there. You read the postscript at the bottom of it, right?" Steph asked.

Darcy glanced at the very bottom of the scroll.

"P.S. It's bad news."

STEVE

Surrounded by mecha-moles, Steve threw a power punch at one of them. The mole used its silver claws to grip Steve by the wrist and fling him onto the floor. It tried to drop a knee on Steve's stomach, but Steve rolled away and kicked that mole right on its rear end, stunning it.

He saw Three running on the wall, two mecha-moles in his path. Three spun like a tornado and drove his feet into the first mecha-mole, who went crashing back into the second. They hit the ground and ran away.

"If you're strong enough, Ninja Steve, you don't have to worry about striking a weak point," Three said.

Steve thought about that, then decided to stick with his own strategy. He knew an effective way to fight, the way that Sensei Raheem had taught him: kick their butts.

Steve dispatched one more mecha-mole with a spinning back-kick. Three drove the last of the mecha-moles out of the room, leaving Steve alone with him. The room itself was wrecked. Holes in the wall. Gouges in the floor. Nothing was where it was supposed to be.

"Who are you and what do you want?" Steve asked the masked man.

"Calm down," Three said. "I'm not here to start a fight with you."

"I'm not going to be calm. In case you didn't notice, we're under attack!" Steve said, the meaning of it fully sinking into his brain.

"It happens," Three said. "Anyway, isn't your sister supposed to be in one of the nearby buildings?"

Steve pounded one of his fists into his own palm. "You'd better stay away from my sister. She's gotten stronger since last time."

Three shrugged. "Once again, I'm not here to fight her. Which building would she be…?"

The man trailed off and looked at his watch. Steve noticed that it was very similar to the one Darcy used to wear.

"What does that watch do?" Steve asked.

"It reminds you that time's always running out," Three said, tapping on his watch. Neon ones and zeroes came pouring out of it and formed a puddle on the floor. Three stepped into it, and the puddle vanished the moment he was gone. Steve knelt down and touched the floor. It was freezing cold.

When Steve stood back up, he was facing a female ninja in a red uniform. He gave a quick shout and hopped away from her.

Ever since he had used Queen Trissa's spell of melted time in Botsylvania, Steve had received occasional visits from the red ninja. She never spoke, and Steve hoped that it would stay that way.

Her uniform told him enough about her. In the earliest days of Ninjastoria, Overlord Ninja Winthrop had issued a decree that all criminal ninjas would have to wear crimson uniforms as a sign of their criminal status. The rule had stuck around, and if a ninja "went red," it was a big deal.

The red ninja stood with her arms crossed. As usual, Steve did his best to ignore her. He found his copy of Sensei Raheem's book and read a page on why every ninja should learn to play soccer because it would improve kicking skills while building teamwork.

Steve looked up from the book, and the red ninja motioned for him to get up and walk down the hall. Then she disappeared.

There was no way he was walking out of his cell. He wasn't about to risk being labeled a runaway. Sooner or later, one of the guards would come by. The fighting, from what he could tell, was over.

His curiosity was building, though. If he got up and poked his head out, what would be there?

No. He would not give in. He was going to be a better ninja from this day forward. He was going to obey the law. He was...

"Ninja Steve!" barked Sensei Raheem's voice from the

intercom.

The speaker box had been damaged in the fight; it was dangling from the ceiling.

"Why are you sitting there? Get yourself to the cafeteria right now! It's a clear path."

Steve leaped to his feet, held Sensei Raheem's book tight against his side, and stepped into the hall. Sure enough, it was wrecked. Holes dug in the ground, scorch marks everywhere, and throwing knives stuck in the walls and the water fountain. There was even a gold-handled spear lying on the ground. Steve left it there.

He ran along the wall in order to avoid all of the holes in the ground. From the looks of it, a brute mecha-mole had been in with the pack of scouts. There were tunnel entrances that were gigantic.

When Steve reached the cafeteria, he found Sensei Raheem dispatching a mecha-mole by picking it up and rolling it like a bowling ball into the rest of its companions. Sensei Raheem was in a smoke-colored uniform that was only a few shades lighter than his skin. He carried a black, wooden baseball bat slung across his back, exactly like a sword. His short mohawk had gotten messed up in the fight and he was trying to readjust it.

"Ninja Steve, I'm here to tell you that President Ninja has

ended your prison term early," said Sensei Raheem.

Steve nodded. "Thank you. What about Nora?"

"Since you two are the only prisoners in all of Ninjastoria, it makes sense to get both of you out of here," he said.

The prison was so quiet that Steve was even more uneasy than before. If there were battle sounds, he could at least know that there was danger up ahead. With everything so quiet, there was too much room for a surprise.

"Sensei, are we at war?" Steve asked.

"We are about to be, Ninja Steve," said his teacher.

"Why would the moles start a war?"

"I guess you haven't gotten to the part of my book about war, have you?" he said, gesturing at the book in Steve's hand. "I hate to make it sound simple—because war is never simple, Ninja Steve. The short version is that The Mole Republic is still angry that we defeated the Mole Emperor. Even worse, it led to a brief collapse of their country while Prince Eldin and Princess Drogar fought for leadership. Once they finished battling each other, everything got sorted out, and Eldin took charge. Now, they're united and they're most likely here for revenge."

"Prince Eldin? Never heard of him," said Ninja Steve.

Sensei Raheem sighed, pulled a tomato out of his back pocket, and crushed it against the top of Steve's head. "Ninja Steve,

17

there was a written journal homework for my History of the Ninja Wars class. I should make you redo the assignment when this war is over."

Steve wiped some of the tomato juice out of his eyes. He felt that he actually deserved that one, so he didn't protest. Plus, he was impressed that his sensei could somehow keep a tomato in his back pocket for an entire battle without crushing it.

"Sensei, why did Prince Eldin have to fight Princess Drogar?" he asked.

"Why don't you ask him that right now?" said his sensei. "He's standing right behind us."

DARCY

If you looked at it from the right spot, the chemistry building was shaped exactly like the periodic table. There were 150 classrooms, one for each element that already existed, plus room for the next twenty that had yet to be discovered or created. In class, Sensei Poh-Shen had given a lecture about how some ninjas felt that the discovery of stealthium and bubblegumium marked the end of elemental discovery. Sensei Poh-Shen herself said that she wasn't willing to make such a bold declaration.

Ninja Steph was supposed to meet her, but it was already 6:56 and there was no sign of her. Darcy climbed the rope ladder up to the fourth floor and then passed through the secret bookcase to get to where the teacher offices were.

Sensei Poh-Shen's door was shaped like a beaker. She had a poster on the door that said, "The Most Important Element is the Element of Surprise."

Darcy knocked. She waited. She knocked again. She waited again.

"Hello? Sensei? It's Marcy. I'm here to see you."

Nothing. Darcy knocked two more times, then left. When she exited the building, she saw Ninja Steph and her best friend, Ninja Kelly, sitting on a bench. Ninja Steph pointed at her and then she and Kelly both started cracking up.

Darcy felt a familiar fire awaken inside of her. She knew that it had to do with the ghost spirit that she carried within. Currently, the fire was telling her to march over to the two girls who had played a prank on her.

"What is wrong with you?!" Darcy barked, shocking herself with the edge in her voice.

That only made Steph laugh harder. "Because you're so gullible."

Darcy ground her teeth together. She had to overpower her anger. She had to tame it.

"What's the matter, Marcy? Have you finally realized that you're never going to be a real ninja like us?" Steph smiled.

Ninja Kelly, however, had stopped laughing.

"At least one of you is smart enough to feel scared," said Darcy.

"Oh? Is this about intimidation?" asked Steph. "I'll have you know that my mother, Ninja Wendi, is one of the best ninja lawyers around. If you hurt me, I'll sue you for everything you're worth."

Darcy laughed. She had no money, no property. She was worth nothing. Even so, she knew it wasn't worth striking Ninja Steph. Instead, Darcy turned and walked away.

She was not followed.

She knew she needed to find a good place to calm down, so she walked through the Field of Tall Purple Grass and then made a left turn in order to get to the Crystal Wind Chime Wall. Gertie had taken her here once before, on a day when she was really feeling down about the bureau's decision to expel her.

A winding path took her down through a tunnel, where a playful breeze guided her forward and led her out into a wide circle filled with stone benches. All around her was a cylindrical wall of solid crystal that went up and up. It was as if someone had carved the crystal so that it looked like a drinking straw for giants. There were patches of green and swirls of fiery red and the occasional spots of pink. The color wasn't what made the place special, though.

It was the music.

The wind that ran with her through the tunnel came whipping out into the middle of it all, and that was what made the music happen. A soft whistle, a gentle hum, and something that almost sounded like a soothing "laaaaa" filled her ears.

According to Gertie, no one knew who had done it, but some ninja had carved holes in parts of the crystal wall, so that when the wind rushed over it, the entire cavern would fill with peaceful notes.

Darcy sat on the ground, rested her back against one of the

stone benches, and let the soft singing of the wind ease her thoughts.

"This isn't so bad," said a voice inside her head.

Toran had gone completely silent since he spoke to her in Botsylvania.

"I didn't know you'd care about music," Darcy thought.

"Every creature loves music."

"Why weren't you like this when we first encountered you?" Darcy asked.

"Being sealed up in a vase for years will fill you with rage."

"Right," Darcy thought, and then she remembered that even if Toran was enjoying the music, he had been considered dangerous enough that the ninjas had sent Steve's parents and her parents to capture him all those years ago. *"So, do you get to know all of my thoughts now?"*

"No. You can't read any of mine, can you?"

She couldn't.

"How does this work, then?" she asked. *"You haven't spoken in weeks."*

"I'm not sure. There's a magic at work here that I know nothing about. I think that masked man did something."

"His name is Three," Darcy thought. *"I don't know what he wants out of all of this. I know that he isn't any good."*

"Hmmmm," Toran mused.

"How do I set you free?" Darcy asked.

She waited thirty seconds before realizing that she would not be receiving a response. Toran had vanished again.

Darcy let the music wash over her. She did a few sets of meditative breathing before walking out and heading back to Gertie's house. Along the way, the paths were empty and the streets were whisper-quiet. In a way, she felt that it was how a ninja village was meant to be: seemingly empty and silent. Yet, after living here, she knew it meant something was terribly wrong.

When she got home, Ninja Gertie and her husband, Ninja Morris, were both seated on the ceiling in their rocking chairs.

"Have you heard the news?" Gertie asked.

Darcy shook her head.

"The mecha-moles dug into Ninjastoria and attacked. This was probably a quick test of our defenses, but in a little while, I'm sure they'll throw everything they've got at us."

Cold dread filled Darcy. If the mecha-moles were here, it meant that they had beaten the Bureau of Sneakery. And if they were powerful enough to do that, then what chance did Ninjastoria have?

"Is...is there anything I should do?" Darcy asked.

"We're going to need all of the ninjas we can get in order to defend our country," Gertie said.

"I'll try to help you, then."

"No, Marcy, that's not good enough," Gertie said. "You're not going to try to help. You're going to help us *win*."

Darcy stood a little taller. "Yes, sensei."

"Tomorrow morning, Marcy I'm accelerating your training. You'll be standing on the ceiling in no time, and that will be the *least* impressive thing you can do."

All her life, Darcy had felt the only place she would ever belong would be the Bureau of Sneakery. Now, a new sense of pride filled her from head to toe.

It was time to dig deeper, to make better use of every minute, and to put every ounce of her energy into becoming a full-fledged ninja.

STEVE

Steve stared at Prince Eldin.

The prince's green skin had flecks of gold in it and his mechanical claws were golden, to match. Prince Eldin was a towering, powerful figure, almost twice as tall as Sensei Raheem. Unlike the scouts, he wore full battle armor: a scratched-up golden helmet, black and gold boots, and a chest plate that was covered in dents from previous fights. In his hands, he carried a long pole with a drill bit on each end.

"Go on," said the prince, looking down at Steve as if he was a beetle. "Ask me the question that's on your mind."

"Who's standing behind you?" Steve asked.

It was not the question that Prince Eldin was expecting. Standing behind him, however, was a forest-green mecha-mole who was a full head taller than Steve, yet way shorter than Eldin. The armor on this mole was a dull brown, as opposed to the prince's flashy gold, and he wore glasses that clipped across his snout.

"I am—" started the smaller mole.

"This is my son and the heir to the throne of The Mole Republic," said Eldin. "Prince Elom."

Steve noticed that Elom's armor was completely unscathed. It was a curious contrast to his father's.

"I've never been friends with a prince," said Steve. "Elom, we should be friends."

Elom shuddered at the suggestion. "Friends? With a monster like you?"

Steve bristled. No one had ever called him a monster. A distraction or a nuisance or a fructose frog-licker, sure. Never a monster, though.

Eldin put an end to their exchange. "My son's only connection to the ninjas will be defeating them in battle and taking control of Ninjastoria once it has fallen."

Steve looked at Eldin, then at Elom, who adjusted his glasses and shifted his weight from side to side.

"It looks to me like Elom is nervous about that," thought Steve.

Sensei Raheem cleared his throat. He rolled his hand around in the air, gesturing for Eldin to get on with it. Steve also noticed that Sensei Raheem was holding a fresh tomato.

"Raheem, I can hear the spirit of my father calling on me to destroy you," said Eldin. "So, here we go."

He struck with his drill spear at the exact same time that Sensei Raheem threw his tomato. The fruit burst apart the moment it hit the spear, splattering red juice and tomato guts right into Eldin's face.

Steve turned his attention to Prince Elom, who was taking

small steps his way. Perhaps this was a trick to disguise his true warrior capacity. Let the enemy underestimate you, then totally overwhelm him.

"Okay, ninja," said Elom. "Today will be your last day of eating cooked ninja meat. I hope you enjoyed your breakfast, you cannibal."

Steve was so shocked by this comment that when Elom threw a punch, Steve didn't move to block it. Lucky for Steve, Elom's sloppy punch didn't hurt at all.

"Haha!" said Elom. "Your martial arts are no match for mine. I bet that you regret not eating more fried ninja for breakfast."

Steve shook his head. What was this kid talking about? What kind of bizarre dream was this? Surely, this had to be a dream.

The young prince opened his claws and Steve snapped back to attention. Even a light graze from those would hurt.

"We don't eat fried ninja. That would be gross. Plus, eating fried stuff isn't healthy," he said.

Steve dodged a claw swipe and elbowed Elom's battle armor. Immediately, Steve regretted it. He had hit his funny bone and there was absolutely nothing funny about it.

The prince yelped and dropped to the ground, clutching his stomach. He rolled around.

"Help!" he shouted. "Dad, he's going to capture me and make

me a slave and force me to cook ninja stew for their evil schools in the mornings!"

Sensei Raheem, who was busy trying to avoid Prince Eldin's spear attacks, roared with laughter. "That's right, Steve! Remember, we need as much help with the stew as we can get, especially for tomorrow. We have a lot of our own people to cook, so don't you dare let him escape!"

Prince Elom clasped his claws together. "I can't believe you cheated in order to defeat me!"

In a flash, Prince Eldin abandoned his fight with Sensei Raheem. He scooped up his son and backed off.

"Incredible," said Eldin. "This ninja student of yours had to stoop to cheating in order to defeat my son. Raheem, this is disgraceful."

Sensei Raheem crossed his arms.

"Tell President Ninja he has five days to surrender to me and my forces," said Eldin.

The prince and his son dug into the earth and vanished in a spray of dirt and rocks, leaving behind a very confused Ninja Steve and a very amused Sensei Raheem.

"Sensei, did I get a concussion?" asked Ninja Steve. "Because I have no idea what's going on. He accused us of being cannibals. Then, I hit that kid once and he collapsed and accused me of not fighting fair. That can't be right."

Sensei Raheem gave Steve a thumbs-up. "That was exactly what you should expect from fighting a spoiled prince, Ninja Steve. His father thinks the boy is a great warrior, yet you have proven that Prince Elom is, in fact, a real marshmallow. I cannot wait to share this information with the Ninja War Council of War Stuff."

It gave Steve a thought. Was Elom actually a spoiled brat? Was he actually a wimp? What if he wasn't into fighting? Or what if he was much better at solving crossword puzzles? Steve made a promise to himself to find out more about the young prince.

"Sensei Raheem," Steve asked, "is there really going to be a war?"

His teacher's expression darkened. "You know I won't lie to you, Ninja Steve. There is a ninety-nine percent chance that we'll go to war. Prince Eldin doesn't like to negotiate and President Ninja won't surrender. The moles will attack in five days, so do lots of stuff that makes you happy. Or, if you're really scared of something, face your fear, like it says in chapter twenty-three of my book."

Sensei Raheem made sure that Steve got back to his house. Before Steve went inside, though, he flipped through the book until he found chapter twenty-three. It was a short one.

Sensei Raheem wrote that in order to make war less scary, it helped to do something that really scared you.

Steve thought for a while and after a few minutes, he had figured out exactly what scary thing he wanted to do.

DARCY

In the morning, Darcy, Gertie, and Morris all gathered around the television to watch President Ninja's speech.

President Ninja wore his own version of a military outfit. His black uniform had three metal moustache pins on each of his shoulders. They were white, purple, and green.

"Each pin stands for a different act of valor," said Gertie. "Although, rumor has it that some of those acts of valor include card tricks and knock-knock jokes."

There was a sinking feeling in Darcy's stomach. President Ninja was hard to take seriously sometimes, which made today's event feel extra strange.

He stood in front of a plain white background. There was no podium. It was only President Ninja, his decorated uniform, his presidential moustache pinned to the outside of his mask, and his words.

"My fellow ninjas, many of you lived through our first clash with the mecha-moles. You know that we fought battles on their territory, not ours. You know of the heroism that resulted in the defeat of the Mole Emperor and the retreat of his armies. Even so, it was an ugly, ugly war.

"There are children in Ninjastoria who are either too young to remember the war or have been lucky enough to grow up in a world that hasn't seen war in a long time. I am sorry to say that war has returned."

For the first time, Darcy saw President Ninja as a normal person. This somber news was hurting his heart and it was as clear as crystallium.

"Prince Eldin, the current leader of The Mole Republic, appeared in Ninjastoria last night. He was met by none other than Sensei Raheem. He told Raheem that we had five days to surrender before he directed his army to attack us.

"Because Prince Eldin is not available for follow-up questions, I do not know if yesterday counted as day one. We have to assume that today is day two. What I do know is that all of Ninjastoria's battle squads will need to meet at noon today.

"The mecha-moles will not have to attack our borders. They will be able to burrow right underneath of us and attack wherever they please. The mecha-moles are also able to eat metal, so I recommend that all ninjas find their baseball bats, bo staffs, bokken, and other wooden weapons. Remember the old saying: 'Sticks and stones may break some bones, but so will baseball bats, bo staffs, bokken, and other wooden weapons.'

"The youth of Ninjastoria—anyone still in high school and younger—should report to the school soccer field on day five. There, Sensei Chow and an entire battle squad of four hundred ninjas will establish a protected zone. As in previous wars, students twelve and up may volunteer for certain non-combat jobs.

"We will not surrender and we will not be defeated. We will stand together and we will remind the mecha-moles that Ninjastoria is a symbol of goodness and hope and righteousness."

Then, the Ninjastoria national anthem, "Independent Ninjas" by Shinobi-Onsay, played.

Ninja Gertie turned off the television. Morris was silent, as usual. Darcy felt empty. The moles had really done it. They had beaten the Bureau of Sneakery's female campus. Her old home.

"Marcy, you can take the next five minutes to feel sad and lost," said Gertie. "After that, it's time to get you a baseball bat and get back to walking on the walls."

Darcy stood up. "I don't need five minutes. Let's get back to work."

STEVE

Steve's dad turned off the television after President Ninja's war speech. Nora and Mom sat on the sofa. Steve was sitting on the floor, trying to make sense of what he had witnessed.

Last night, the house had been full of happiness. Minutes after Steve had walked in the door, Nora had arrived home from jail, and the whole family was reunited.

Nora had told her parents that she loved them and that she was sorry for disappointing them. She gave Steve the biggest hug she had ever given him.

After that, she had quickly changed out of her red uniform and joined them in the kitchen for dinner prep.

They'd made pasta with a spicy tomato sauce and fresh basil, and Nora had baked her almost-famous garlic bread: crispy and crusty on the outside, yet pillowy-soft in the center.

For the entire evening, everything had felt good and right. But this morning's speech from President Ninja flattened the mood.

Gather weapons. Prepare for war. Mecha-moles attacking anywhere, any time.

"I thought war was supposed to...you know...have more order to it. Like, the sides would agree where to battle and how many soldiers to bring," Steve said.

His mom shook her head. "It's mostly chaos, Steve."

Steve stood up and began to pace. What if the mecha-moles were tunneling beneath their house at this very moment? Or what if they had already dug tunnels under all of Ninjastoria and would make it collapse? How was anyone going to get anything done over the next few days?

His mom tried again. "Steve, there are thousands and thousands of ninjas here. We have weapons and techniques and training for defending our homeland. You've had training, too. This will be over quickly and the moles will run away."

All of that seemed believable. It helped a little bit.

"Now, do you know where your baseball bat is?" his dad asked. "Or do you prefer your bo staff?"

"Bat," Steve muttered. "But first..."

If war was coming, then he needed to do something scary, like Sensei Raheem had recommended.

Thirty minutes later, he stood on the door step to Ninja Gertie's. He stared at the door. He was sweating. He tried to knock and couldn't.

"Oh, man," he said. "This is tough. Fine, I'll knock on the count of four. One, two—"

The door swung open. Ninja Gertie was standing there with her arms crossed.

"State your business," she said.

"I…um…I'm here to…" Steve started. He was regretting his decision to face one of his fears. He hadn't considered that he would have to face Ninja Gertie, too.

Gertie shook her head. "I don't know why I even bother. Marcy!"

Steve watched as Darcy came running. She had on a blue apron and there was a light dusting of flour on it. There was also a light dusting of flour on her freckled cheeks.

"Yes, sensei?" she asked.

Gertie gestured at Steve. "This young man is here and he won't tell me why. When you've finished talking, let's get those pies in the oven. It's almost noon, so Morris and I have to go meet our battle squads soon."

With that, Gertie walked away. Steve was silent for a moment, until he was sure that she was gone.

"Wow, she's intimidating," said Steve.

"You don't know the half of it," said Darcy. "What brings you here?"

Steve swallowed. "Well, I was thinking…so, if there's going to be a war and lots of fighting and stuff…I…I was wondering if you'd want to hang out and get ice cream at Fro-Zen tomorrow night."

There. He had said it. The words had left his mouth and he

couldn't take them back.

"Sure!" she said. "I'll be done with dinner and training tomorrow at 7. Can I meet you there at 7:45?"

"Yeah," said Steve.

Ninja Gertie called from far away. "Marcy! It's time to get back to baking."

"Gotta run," Darcy said.

"See you later," said Steve.

She shut the door and then it was done. Steve walked away. Then, he ran. He ran straight to Samurai Sam's house.

Sam and his family lived in a house specifically made for the ambassador from Bushido Gardens. It was designed to look like a samurai temple, with wide, tall doors and a roof that curved upward at the corners, so that it kind of looked like it was smiling. They even had a statue in the front yard of a flying armadillo — the revered, armored animal that carried samurai into battle.

Sam and his dad, Karl, were fixing armored plates over the windows on the main level. Sam was holding one in place while his dad was using a drill to secure it to the window frame. Neither of Sam's parents had a battle squad meeting to attend, because they weren't citizens of Ninjastoria.

"The mecha-moles eat metal," said Steve, barely louder than

the drill. "Is this worth it?"

Sam's dad frowned. "Mecha-moles have stomachs, Ninja Steve. Eventually, stomachs get full. These armored plates will be perfect."

Sam asked his dad if he could take a break to talk to Steve. He was granted two minutes.

"You look happy, Steve. Suspiciously happy. Everything okay?"

Steve told Sam what had happened. Sam gave him a high-five. Then, Sam had to go back to helping his dad with the windows.

Steve texted Arjun to see if he was home.

"Sorry, Steve. At the arcade with my sister while our parents are at the battle meeting."

That made sense. Arjun's little sister was a pro gamer. Although she was only seven years old, she was seriously skilled in *Colossal Crashers: Turbo Edition* and had won the Ninjastoria tournament for two years in a row. Steve had played against her once and she had defeated him in under thirty seconds. He imagined that Arjun was probably getting beaten just as badly.

Steve passed the rest of the afternoon helping out around the house. His parents left a note asking him and Nora to put two tennis ball launchers on the roof of the house. Instead of filling the ammo chambers with regular tennis balls, though, they cut slits in the tennis balls and filled them with itching powder and sneezing powder. Getting hit with a tennis ball was annoying, sure, but getting covered in itching powder and sneezing powder made fighting practically impossible.

Nora and Steve handled dinner so that it would be ready when their parents got home. They decided on breakfast foods, so Nora pulled the ingredients to whip up a big batch of cinnamon-honey waffle batter and Steve started cracking a dozen eggs.

"How was jail for you?" Steve asked.

"Way too boring," said Nora. "I did a lot of working out. I'm developing a new technique, too. It's going to be something worth unveiling at the Unlimited Power Tournament in Bushido Gardens."

"If it doesn't get cancelled by mecha-mole war," Steve said. It was a dark thought.

The Unlimited Power Tournament happened every five years in a different country, except for the years when a war kept them apart. Ordinarily, representatives from many different countries would show up for a non-lethal battle tournament that was meant to celebrate the variety of fighting styles that came from all over.

Steve let a moment of silence go by.

"Nora, did Three show up on the day that the moles first appeared?" Steve asked.

"Nope," she said. "Where'd that question come from?"

Steve started scrambling the eggs. "He came to my cell, helped me fight off some moles, and then said he was going to find you."

Nora shook her head. "I never saw him."

After that, Steve let the matter drop. Nora took the lead in the conversation, asking all about his days in his cell.

Their parents got back at six, looking serious. Steve's dad didn't laugh at all during dinner, not even when Steve said, "Dad, isn't dinner egg-cellent?"

Steve tried not to take it personally.

While he was doing the dishes, he was thinking of what he should say to Darcy. First, he wanted to know what kind of training Ninja Gertie was putting her through. Then, he wanted to know what kinds of pies they had been baking.

Tomorrow night was going to be great.

"Well," Steve thought, *"as long as the mecha-moles don't find a way to ruin everything."*

DARCY

A day later—day three of five—and still she couldn't manage to stand on a wall or the ceiling for more than a second. Hours of falling. Hours of failing.

"This is ridiculous!" Darcy shouted as she fell once again. She was getting worse with each attempt.

"Control that temper," Gertie commanded. "How were you ever an agent?"

Darcy looked right back at her. "I'm an exchange student from the Valley of Fallen Stars."

"Sure, and I'm from the dinosaur assassin army. Who do you think you're fooling, Marcy?"

She stared at her fingers. "My temper's been getting out of hand ever since…"

At this, Gertie raised her eyebrows. "Ever since what?"

Darcy sighed and rolled up her sleeve, revealing her tiger stripes. "Ever since I got this ghost curse."

Gertie sighed. "That's a tattoo, meant to build up your backstory so that you don't seem like an agent. If it was a true ghost curse, Marcy, you'd be a ghost by now. Take a break and clear your mind."

Darcy was left alone in the training room. She sat down and slumped back against the wall. What if it took months to connect to the energy in Ninjastoria? That wasn't an option. She needed to get there *now*. She needed to be able to get it done so that she could make Steph and Kelly leave her alone.

Also, it was six o'clock, which meant that there wasn't much time until she was supposed to meet Steve for ice cream. That was bringing about its own kind of stress. A lot of the time they'd spent together was while they were dealing with big problems. Then, the moment she'd been welcomed back into Ninjastoria, Ninja Steve had been put in jail.

Something told her that, "What was jail like?" wasn't going to lead to a good conversation with Steve. Plus, what could he ask *her* about? She couldn't talk about agent stuff, since that was all top-secret.

This did not seem like it was going to go well.

Darcy wished that she could call Matilda and ask her for advice. Then she realized that she'd never see Matilda again. Or, if she did, Matilda would deny it in order to keep her cover.

"That was the past," Darcy whispered. "The past is gone and this is your life now."

Gertie came back at six thirty, before Darcy could settle her thoughts. If anything, she was even more stressed out after her break than before it.

"Let's try standing on the ceiling once more. It's only a matter of time before you can feel the energy flowing through Ninjastoria, I swear," said Gertie. "Picture the energy in your imagination and lock onto that image."

The only energy Darcy felt was the bubbling anger that she knew was coming from Toran's ghost curse. Maybe that was the issue: she was so tuned-in to the ghost part of herself that she couldn't possibly sense the magic that allowed the ninjas to stand on the ceiling or perform their techniques.

Darcy faced the wall. She planted her left foot against it. In her head, she pictured bolts of blue energy forking down from her heart and into her ankles, spreading out through her toes.

The sole of her foot felt toasty, then, like she was standing barefoot on sun-warmed sand. Not at all like the heat from her ghost fire.

Now, for the other foot. Her heartrate spiked.

Darcy felt both of her feet humming with energy. When she lifted her right foot off of the ground, she didn't fall. Inch by inch, she moved it toward the wall.

The wall exploded.

Darcy was shot back like a bullet, but Gertie caught her and set her on her feet.

Two brute mecha-moles walked through the destruction. These ones were each six feet tall and wore green and black armor. They had green goggles on and their metal claws were different from any she had seen before. These ones had seven fingers instead of five and they had glowing lines running from palm to fingertips.

"Prince Eldin said we'd have five days," said Darcy. "This is day three, isn't it?"

"Yes, well, it appears that the prince is a liar," said Gertie, who looked the moles over from head to foot. "Since you two moles have come knocking, you've reminded me of a classic joke: Knock, knock."

"Who's there, old crone?" said one of the mecha-moles.

Darcy didn't know all of the ninja techniques by name just yet. But if she had to put a name to what Gertie did, she would have called it, "the spell of immediate need for medical attention."

The floor beneath that mecha-mole suddenly acted like a trampoline and it flung him into the air. Gertie became a blur, reappearing only when she was in the air right in front of that very surprised mecha-mole. She drove a palm deep into its belly, then picked it up over her head and threw it down into the ground. The mecha-mole landed on its back and the impact left a crater in the ground.

It lay there and said, "I surrender."

The other mole looked at Gertie. He pointed a clawed finger at her.

Darcy realized that she had an opening. If she could activate her bolt-boots, then she...but, no, she didn't have those anymore. All she had was...

She snapped her fingers and the lava-hot flash of ghost fire rippled across her palm. The giant mecha-mole stopped looking at Gertie.

Darcy bent her knees, gave a power shout like Gertie had taught her, and ran straight at her enemy. The mecha-mole blocked her fire punch, but its metal claw melted on contact, revealing a much smaller black claw beneath it.

Gertie hit the mecha-mole with a leg-sweep and it landed flat on its back. Before it could do anything, Gertie grabbed it by the ankles, swung it in a circle, and hurled it into the other mecha-mole, who was just starting to get to his feet.

They collided, rolled around, and then the two moles started digging through the floor. Wood splintered, dirt fountained up, and both of them were gone.

Gertie's husband, Ninja Morris, appeared a moment later, holding a pie in each hand. He looked at Gertie and Darcy, then at the wrecked room. Darcy noticed how calm he was, like this sort of thing happened all the time.

"Perhaps," Darcy thought, *"it* does *happen all the time."*

"It's okay, honey, the mecha-moles broke their word and attacked us early," Gertie said. "Thankfully, Marcy was here to help me fight off the two bullies that showed up. Can you bring me the phone, dear? I need to make an important call."

Morris nodded. He left and returned a minute later with the one cell phone that the two of them shared. Gertie took it from him.

"Hello," she said. "Sensei Raheem, this is Ninja Gertie. The mecha-moles have just attacked my house. Oh? What's that? Yes. I understand. I'll do that *and* I'll bring the pies."

Darcy was staring at the hole where the mecha-moles had first come in. It was now a wide, ragged window to the outside world. Through it, Darcy saw smoke rising throughout Ninjastoria.

"Marcy," said Gertie. "Before we leave, I want to say that I've seen a lot of things in my life. I've *never* seen a person use ghost fire. I apologize for not believing you."

Darcy gulped. "Please don't tell anyone."

Gertie *tsked*. "Hide whatever you want about your personal life or where you're from, Marcy. But if I can only teach you one thing, I want to teach you to be proud of everything that makes you strong."

There was relief, mixed with shame.

"Marcy, we're at war, and I have a very specific responsibility. I need you to get yourself a baseball bat from the garage, some shuriken, and the big backpack that I use for delivering pies to my friends."

"Absolutely. Are you sure I can come long?"

Gertie smiled. "Oh, I'm quite sure. You definitely belong with us at our gathering. I'm sure they'll make you a member in no time."

"A member? Of what?" Darcy asked.

"The Sisterhood of Butt-Kicking."

STEVE

The next day was more war prep for the adult battle squads. Steve did his best to remain calm. Nora even helped him with an hour-long meditation session.

After dinner, Steve told his parents that he was going to Sam's. He didn't want anyone — especially Nora — knowing that he was actually going into town for ice cream with Darcy.

He thought about what he was going to order. Fro-Zen was known for its ice cream rolls that looked like sushi rolls. The Triple Trio was vanilla, chocolate, and strawberry ice cream sculpted so that each piece looked like a cut of tuna roll. Of course, there was also the Mango Tango, which used vanilla and mango ice cream to look like pieces of tamago sushi.

As Steve reached the mirror maze, he was still debating what to get.

Had he looked behind him, he would have seen the giant, spinning drill missile that had been launched. Had he been a little less excited about hanging out with Darcy, he would have heard the low whistle that it made as it cut through the sky.

He wasn't. He didn't.

There was a huge, crackling explosion that knocked Steve off of his feet and left him wondering how he had ended up on the ground.

He propped himself up with his left arm, then his right.

It suddenly smelled like a campfire, and not the kind where s'mores were being made.

"What happened?" Steve asked.

Every single mirror panel that he could see had been cracked or broken.

There was laughter from behind him. Steve whirled around and found a squad of twenty scout mecha-moles standing there on their hind legs. Unlike before, however, these ones were wearing full suits of green metal armor. Their claw hands were equipped with spinning drills and their heavy boots had wheels on them.

"Your prince promised that we'd have five days!" Steve shouted. "Now you've broken a promise, ruined our maze, and probably ruined my ice cream date!"

The mecha-mole in front said, "Too bad."

Steve knew that he had no chance of beating all of them. He was scared, but he was not scared to admit that he was scared.

Steve repeated Sensei Raheem's maxim: "Admit that you feel fear, then face it."

He had no shuriken. No katana. Nothing but his fists, his feet, the spell of shadow taming, and the spell of melted time.

Five of the moles jumped Steve at once. He did a back

handspring and avoided the initial attack. The moment his feet touched the ground, he did a split, and a diving mecha-mole went right over his head.

He sprang back up and delivered a knuckle-sandwich to the only opening in the mecha-mole's armor: the face.

His joy was short-lived. Sure enough, one of them grabbed him from behind. Another socked him right in the stomach.

"Oof!" said Steve.

"Hey!" came a shout. "The only one who gets to beat him up is *me*."

Nora came jetting down from the sky. She was in her usual black uniform, but this time she was wearing a yellow armband around her right elbow.

The mecha-moles immediately let go of Steve and he did a jumping double back-kick that sent the one behind him tumbling away. The kick catapulted Steve forward and he landed next to his sister.

"You okay, little brother?" she asked.

"I'm better now," he said.

"I hope these moles are ready to fight two of Ninjastoria's most notorious criminals," she said, handing Steve one of her katanas.

Nora unclipped two pairs of nunchakus from her belt. They

were made of tan swiftwood, perfectly smooth and perfectly dangerous. Soon, they were nothing but a blur, and Nora started smacking mole after mole.

Steve gripped the katana and relaunched his attack.

"Nora, what are we supposed to do? There are so many of them," he said, his sword clashing with the drill bit of a scout. "Plus, don't they eat metal?"

As Steve finished speaking, the mecha-mole ripped the katana out of his hands and devoured the blade in two chomps.

"We have to hold out for one more minute. Then the rest of the squad will arrive," Nora said.

The moles were zipping around on their wheeled boots, and they dashed at Steve and Nora, forcing them back.

"Fine!" she said. She cracked her knuckles, whistled low, and tugged on her lower lip. One of her nunchaku now looked like a set of oversized baseball bats chained together.

"Batter up!" she shouted and, with a mighty swing, she sent five of the moles soaring at once.

Steve watched as six other ninjas arrived, dropping from the sky on gliders. All of them had a yellow armband around one arm. And all of them were girls or women. Steve recognized his mom among them.

They stepped in unison and then thrust their fists forward.

The ground beneath the remaining mecha-moles turned into a geyser of water and lifted the moles into the air. All of the newcomers then pulled out wooden practice swords—bokken—and struck.

The moles fled after that.

"Let's get moving," one of women said. She was taller than Nora, older than Nora. Her skin was many shades darker, and she had a sledgehammer slung across her back. Steve immediately recognized Ninja Amari, who was famous for winning the Unlimited Power Tournament more times than any other woman *or* man. She was a six-time champion.

Steve followed along as the group bounded through the mirror maze, eventually leaping up onto the top edge of it when they left the damaged section behind. Steve looked back once and saw that the broken glass glittered on the ground like diamonds in the twilight.

In his head, war had been something fought out in the wilderness. It wasn't something that knocked down your front door and wrecked your hometown.

Now he realized that he had been wrong. That was *exactly* what war did. All wars.

His stomach gave a twist.

"Everything's going to be okay," said his mom, who was right in front of him.

"Weren't you supposed to be going to Samurai Sam's? How'd you wind up here?" Nora asked, falling back to Steve's right and keeping pace with him as they ran.

Steve's mother said, "Hmmm."

"I…I was meeting Marcy for ice cream," he said.

Nora patted him on the back. "I'm sorry that your date got ruined, little bro."

Despite her reassurance, Steve still didn't feel well.

"What's up with the yellow armbands?" Steve asked.

"It's our symbol," said Nora. "We are—"

Before Nora could say anything else, something nearby let out a thunderous *boom*.

The walls of the mirror maze collapsed and Steve was falling, falling, falling.

DARCY

Darcy had armed herself with a bat and a handful of shuriken. She went into the kitchen cabinets and—as requested—she pulled out Gertie's special backpack that had five slots in order to hold five pies. When she turned around, Morris had silently arrived and had arranged the pies on the table.

Darcy recognized them immediately. They were the extra-creamy vanilla pudding pies that she and Gertie had made yesterday. Gertie had even taught her the proper way to make a pie crust from homemade graham crackers and fresh-churned butter.

Morris fit all five pies into the backpack and gave Darcy a thumbs-up.

"Thank you, Morris. I guess you're going to stay behind and guard the house?" she asked.

He gave her another thumbs-up.

Gertie was still waiting in the ruined training room. She held out her hands and took the pie backpack from Darcy.

"Since the wall was destroyed, there's no need to use the door," said Gertie, and she led the way out of the house.

Even with pies in tow, Gertie was still light on her feet. They dashed through Ninjastoria as the other ninja battle squads were on their ways to different strategic locations.

In her head, Darcy imagined the same thing must have happened when the Bureau of Sneakery realized it was under attack. She wondered where Natalya and Evelyn would have directed their forces. She wondered if Serena and her parents had been fighting or if they fled. She wondered if the Director had been there at all.

Gertie threw a grappling hook onto the roof of the Ninja News Network television station and scaled the wall that way. Darcy climbed the ladder. She told herself that it was okay to come in second place when racing a senior citizen.

"We've got allies coming this way," Gertie said, pointing at a squad of ninjas running across the top of the mirror maze.

Then there was a deafening boom. Everything around them shook.

Darcy watched as a drill bit the size of a truck went screaming across the sky. It struck the wall of the mirror maze and blasted it into pieces so small that it looked like snow. The ninjas that had been running across it all tumbled down.

"Let's move!" said Gertie.

Gertie leaped off of the roof. It was at least fifty feet off the ground. Darcy remembered what Steve had taught her about falling.

She fell.

The rush of it made her stomach do backflips. She still felt like she was making a terrible mistake.

The moment her foot grazed the ground she rolled and came up running.

"Not bad," said Gertie, who was looking back over her shoulder.

They reached the ruined mirror maze. Darcy saw her broken reflection nearly everywhere she looked.

One after another, the ninjas regrouped. They had all fallen in a way that allowed them to land on their feet.

"Steve?" she asked.

He grumbled as he shook his head. When he turned and saw it was Darcy, he smiled. She smiled back, forgetting to talk.

"Uh...Marcy? You okay?" Steve asked.

She quickly snapped back to reality. "Maybe? I just watched a giant drill missile destroy part of your town. I wonder what Head Ninja Philip III would think."

"He probably would have forced everyone to break all of their mirrors. He was known for doing things that made people hate him, after all," said Steve.

A hand rested on Darcy's shoulder. It was Nora.

"Hey, Marcy, how does it feel to be surrounded by criminals?" Nora asked.

Steve's mother was right behind her and she didn't seem to find Nora's joke to be funny. Both Nora and Nora's mother were wearing yellow armbands tied around one arm. She thought, perhaps, that it was some kind of soldier uniform.

"Stevie, are you cut at all?" asked Ninja Steve's mom.

"Mom, please don't call me that," said Steve, and then added, "I'm injury-free."

"Yeah, Mom, don't embarrass him in front of his girlfriend like that," said Nora, who was clearly intent on making things worse.

Darcy stood there. Years of spy training, weeks of ninja training...yet nothing had taught her how to deal with this. Her hands were clammy, her face was flushed. She had nothing to say. She didn't even know if she should say anything about their cancelled ice cream...hangout? Evening? Date?

It was supposed to be a date, wasn't it?

Thankfully, someone else spoke first.

"Let's go take out that drill cannon," said the woman with the sledgehammer.

Soon, they were all bolting away from the wreckage of the mirror maze and through the main street of downtown Ninjastoria. All of the businesses were closed: Kickin' Cake, Kara-Tea. Even the 24-hour coffee spot, Throwing Star Buck's (named after Ninja Buck, who was really good with shuriken) was shuttered. Darcy assumed that most of the owners were out fighting mecha-moles somewhere.

They found the drill cannon in front of a blocky concrete building that must have been a factory. The hulking cannon had a long, rectangular base that was propped up on three mechanical legs that could each raise and lower, changing the angle at which it would fire the giant drill bits. It made sharp hissing sounds and steam shot out of its sides.

One scout mecha-mole sat in a cockpit that was off to one side. Ten brute mecha-moles were there, too, hustling to reload it.

There was no battle cry. The ninjas silently dashed toward their targets. Darcy stayed close to Nora and Steve's mother.

Ninja Gertie unzipped her pie backpack. Her hands became a blur and she threw all five of the vanilla pudding pies. Each one struck a mecha-mole in the face.

Then, Gertie performed a technique that summoned a cloud of rumble-bees. Ninjastoria's rumble-bees were far worse than regular bumblebees, because they could shoot their stingers like missiles. And, as Darcy had learned in her biology classes, rumble-bees absolutely hated the smell of vanilla.

Like all of the agents, Darcy had been trained to resist

common fears, so she wasn't scared of bees. The mecha-moles, however, didn't seem to have that training.

The cloud of bees attacked the pudding-covered moles and sent them in a panicked run. When one of the brute mecha-moles broke free of the bee cloud, Nora kicked it in the shin. Then, Steve's mom slammed her elbow into its stomach. It went flying toward the metal front doors of the factory and broke right through them.

Darcy ran after it, Nora by her side. The factory was full of clear, teardrop-shaped tanks that were thirty feet high. The tanks were all connected by spiraling silver tubes. Some of them were swirling with dark red liquid, some blue, some golden. All of them had ladders running up the sides.

The mecha-mole had gotten back onto its feet and Darcy drew back for a punch. The mole blocked it with its forearm and swiped at her with its other claw. She felt the claw breeze by her face, barely missing.

"Duck!" shouted Nora.

Darcy ducked just in time for Nora to roundhouse kick the brute mecha-mole. It went flying through the air and struck the tank full of red liquid. There was a crunch and a crackle. The tank burst open and a river of red swept the mecha-mole off of its feet.

A sweet smell filled the factory, but Darcy couldn't quite place it. She shot Nora a quizzical look.

"This is the Juice-Jitsu factory. We're looking at gallons of Choppin' Cherry," Nora said.

The mole approached them once again.

Before Darcy or Nora could strike, a torrent of blue fruit juice shot over their shoulders and blasted the mecha-mole into the wall. Still dripping with juice, it got up, used its claws to dig straight through the wall, and was gone.

Darcy looked behind her and saw Ninja Steve standing on top of one of the tanks. He was holding a fire hose that was connected to the juice tank.

"That was a big dose of vitamin see-you-later!" he shouted.

Darcy grinned. Nora groaned.

"What flavor was that?" Darcy asked.

"Berry Bash!" said Steve. "It's the best one. Want to try it while it's fresh?"

"I'd prefer to wait until I can drink it through a straw, thank you," she said.

They all left the factory and saw that the other ninjas had gained control over the drill cannon. They were tying up unconscious mecha-moles and carrying them off.

"Amari, should we destroy the cannon?" asked Ninja Steve's

mom.

The woman with the sledgehammer hefted it high above her head. "I think that's a fabulous idea."

With a shout, she took three big swings with the hammer. The first side-swing completely destroyed the cockpit. The second side-swing knocked the loaded drill bit off of the front. Finally, Amari's downward swing crushed the steam engine that ran the whole thing.

The ninjas all gave a cheer.

Gertie cleared her throat. "Marcy, I'm sure you've noticed the ladies with the yellow armbands. I would like to introduce you to the Sisterhood of Butt-Kicking."

Darcy made eye contact with all of them. It was clear that Ninja Amari was the one in charge.

Steve leaned in close and whispered, "Ninja Amari is Sensei Raheem's ex-wife. It's been a few years."

Darcy nodded. She didn't know much about Sensei Raheem's personal life. She hadn't even considered if he was married or not.

"Sisterhood, let's get to headquarters and plan our next strike," said Amari. "Ninja Steve, you can come with us, but you can't walk into our base. The sisterhood doesn't allow men to hang out."

Darcy watched Steve deflate. He opened his mouth to say something, then stopped himself.

He turned to Darcy. "It's like the saying from Sensei Raheem's book: never argue with a powerful woman wielding a sledgehammer."

She was impressed. Nora looked stunned. The Steve they had always known would have found it impossible to walk away without a protest. On top of that, he was quoting a book.

"I'll see you soon, Steve," said Darcy. "Be careful, okay?"

"Sure!" said Steve, "I'll—"

There was a crackle of static. Then, it sounded like someone was tapping their fingers against a microphone. Darcy couldn't see any speakers anywhere, but the sound was booming from everywhere at once.

"EVERYONE, SHUT UP! THIS IS IMPORTANT!"

STEVE

The sheer volume of President Ninja's message was enough to make Steve dizzy. He clamped his hands over his ears and braced for the next announcement.

"Ninja squadrons Cheddar, Rapunzel, Thirteen, and Triskaidekaphobia report to station five, immediately," he said. "All ninja students seventeen and under should report to the school grounds immediately. That includes you, Nora!"

"I'm part of the sisterhood," said Nora, to her mother. "I should be with you all, not with the children!"

Steve's mother kept an even tone. "Nora, that was a direct order from President Ninja. He let you out of jail early, in case you forgot. I'm sure that he'll have an important leadership task for you once you get there. Besides, I know that Steve and Marcy will be safe if they travel with you."

Then Steve's mom looked at Steve. "You are doing great, honey. I'm proud of you and I'll tell your dad all about it. He's manning the tennis-ball launchers on top of the house at this very moment."

She gave him a big kiss on the cheek and left in a blur with the rest of the sisterhood. Now it was just him, Darcy, Nora, and a ruined drill cannon. He leaned against the frame of the machine. Darcy walked over and stood across from him.

"This is surreal," Darcy said.

"This is inexcusable!" Nora yelled. "I should be there with the sisterhood. President Ninja keeps treating me like a child."

He thought about telling Nora that she was throwing a temper tantrum, just like a child would. He decided to hold his tongue. Steve watched his sister punch the side of the cannon and leave a deep dent in the side. Nora stormed off, leaving Steve and Darcy alone.

"I know what you mean about it feeling surreal," said Steve. "I had to fight with a juice cannon. I should feel excited about that, but I'm not. I wish I never had to do that."

"War ruins everything," Darcy said. "That's what my main instructor always told me. She was right."

Steve nodded. They were both a bit banged up from the fight and he was grateful for a chance to rest. It also gave him a chance to think. This was war. Real war. It was just getting started.

He had been on top of the mirror maze when it was destroyed. He wondered what else had been wrecked.

Steve didn't feel anything close to the fear he had felt when he was little and scared that the Noogie Monster would be hiding in his closet, waiting to give him a noogie. No, this was a numb, churning kind of fear. It made him realize that some of the things he had been scared of doing weren't anything to be scared of.

"So, Marcy, I...um...I was thinking..." Steve said.

She brushed some of the dirt from her shoulder. "Hm?"

"Once this war is over, I'd still like it if we could — "

Another announcement from President Ninja cut him off. "Ninja squadrons Bagel, Lox, and Cream Cheese all report to station thirty."

Steve didn't try to finish what he had started saying. Darcy didn't ask him to, either. Nora came back. She waved them on, and they began a careful journey to the school grounds as the twilight turned into nighttime.

The fighting hadn't made it that close to the school. They gathered on the soccer field, right by the trampoline section in the center of the field. Steve liked the non-stop chaos of ninja soccer, with its constant trampoline jumping and skateboarding, but this wasn't a good time to play.

"Steve! Marcy! Over here."

Steve ran to Samurai Sam and Ninja Arjun. Arjun's seven-year-old sister was there, too.

Arjun's sister looked at Darcy. "Hello, my name is Priya. My big brother is very tall and one day I am going to be taller than him."

Darcy grinned. "I bet you will."

Steve and Darcy told them about the mirror maze getting blown apart and watched as their happiness faded. But then Steve told them about spraying the mecha-mole with Berry Bash and that brought them back.

"How are you, Marcy?" Arjun asked.

"So far, so good," she said. "Where have you guys been?"

Arjun talked about being at his dad's house and how he and his little sister and his dad had met up with Samurai Sam along the way.

"Sam, what's your dad up to? Did he come here with you?" Steve asked.

"Um…" said Samurai Sam. "Yeah."

Steve knew there was more to the story. He was prevented from finding out because Sensei Chow ushered them into the cafeteria. All of the tables had been pushed aside and over a thousand ninja students formed a mob around their cafeteria master. His bushy eyebrows were dyed in a camouflage pattern and he had two large, wooden cooking spoons crossed over his back. Steve wondered if those were as heavy as the training spatula he had been forced to serve those hamburgers with a few months ago.

"Students, we're at war," he said. "The first war we've had in a long time. I want you to know, before anything else, that it is okay to feel scared. It is okay to cry."

Steve let out a sigh of relief. He noticed that many other students did, too.

Sensei Chow continued. "I don't want anyone here teasing anyone else about how they feel about this war. War takes strength and war takes fighting, yes, but war takes *tears*, too. So when you have the urge to tease someone because they're upset, you need to check yourself. Being a ninja is not about being an unfeeling, brainless soldier. Being a ninja is about sticking together and protecting those who feel vulnerable, not shaming them. Don't forget that."

Steve felt his hands trembling. A few of the students nearby started to sniffle. There was a hand on Steve's back, and it was Darcy's.

Sensei Chow let the silence hang for a moment before continuing. "The laws set in place by Thane Ninja Mariah state that ninjas twelve and older can choose to become part of a war support squad, overseeing the creation or distribution of supplies. Those who wish to stay out of the war can stay here, where a squadron of ninjas is assigned to protect the area."

Steve had already decided to join the support squad. He locked eyes with Darcy and he could tell she would be making the same choice. The rest of the students began to talk to their friends.

"I'm staying here," said Ninja Arjun.

"What?" Steve asked.

Arjun narrowed his eyes. "I'm not taking part in a war, Steve. I'm *twelve*. I'm going to let the adults handle this one while I stay here with my sister."

Steve pulled a breath in through his mouth. It was Arjun's choice. Sensei Chow had told them to support each other, and Steve realized that it needed to start immediately.

"I respect that," Steve said. "I'm joining the support squad."

Darcy said, "Me, too."

Steve looked at Samurai Sam, who pushed his glasses a little higher onto his face. His eyes bounced back and forth between Arjun and Steve.

"I'm going with Steve and Marcy," said Sam.

Before Steve could say anything, he saw that Nora was making a beeline for Sensei Chow. There was fierce hand waving, and Nora looked more and more like she was in a fighting stance.

"Steve, I think we should go try to calm Nora down," said Samurai Sam.

"I think we're too late," Steve said.

DARCY

Darcy saw Nora storming toward Sensei Chow.

That action alone would have gotten her suspended from the agency.

There was no stopping Nora, though. Steve and Sam and Arjun ran after her.

"Oh, look who it is," said Ninja Steph, walking up from behind Darcy. "It's the little ninja who can't."

Darcy clenched her jaw.

"Are you scared, *Marshy*?" she asked, with a smirk.

Ninja Kelly, who was two steps behind her, looked uncomfortable.

"Steph, maybe this isn't—" Kelly started.

"Kelly, if you're my friend, you'll stop talking. I'm talking to Marshy," Steph said, then looked back at Darcy. "I hope you're staying put with the little ones. We don't need anyone out in the field who can't do what's needed."

Darcy said, "You'll need my help."

"With what?" Steph said. "There's nothing you can do that I can't. I have years of ninja training. What do you have? A few weeks? Trust me, Marsh, I'm worth at least five of you."

"You have no idea who I am and what I'm capable of," Darcy said.

Darcy felt like embers were burning inside her palms. That creeping anger was coming back and she knew that she needed to get away from Steph before the anger consumed her.

"We can beat her in a fight, no problem," Toran said, stirring to life in her mind. *"It would be over in five seconds."*

Steph rolled her eyes and walked away just as Steve and Sam and Arjun were coming back.

"Marcy, you look angry," Steve said. "Everything okay?"

"Yeah, I'm fine," Darcy said.

She didn't see much of a point in telling Steve or his friends about Steph and Kelly. What would they be able to do, anyway?

Sensei Chow's discussion with Nora had come to a close. Nora came back, silent.

"Students," Sensei Chow said, "we have drop points where our supplies need to be. If you choose to take part, your only job will be delivering supplies to those locations. Ordinarily, that would be able to keep you clear of most enemy encounters. The reality, though, is that the mecha-moles could be tunneling anywhere they want. Be prepared for fights. Remember their weaknesses: if you encounter a scout, your most effective attack is a kick to the butt. If you encounter a brute mecha-mole, my best advice is to get away from it. Use smoke bombs, oil slicks, whatever you have."

Darcy cleared her throat. "What about royal mecha-moles?"

Sensei Chow's eyebrows went up. "There are only four royal mecha-moles: Empress Dee-Dee, Princess Drogar, Prince Eldin, and Prince Elom. None of them will be part of these attack squads. I guarantee it."

Darcy nodded. Bureau training had taught her that most people performed a certain action when they lied, called a "tic." She had already figured out that Sensei Chow's tic was raising his eyebrows. It made her sad to see a teacher lie, and she wondered why he thought it was necessary.

It was foolish to guarantee anything about those royals, especially since Prince Eldin was looking for revenge for his father, and Drogar would never be one to shy away from combat.

"Now," said Sensei Chow, "If you stay with me, we'll get to the supply depot and hold there until we receive requests from our battle squads."

The supply depot wasn't far from the school. Darcy had passed the small house many times and had never taken notice of it. She supposed that was the point: a rectangular, one-floor, black-roofed house that looked just like any other ninja's house.

There were fifty students who traveled with Sensei Chow and they had to go in the front door of the supply house one at a time. When Darcy got in, she saw that it was anything but an ordinary house.

There was no floor, only a set of stairs going down. A series of pulleys and platforms were there, too, acting as elevators. She walked next to Steve. Sam was right behind them.

When they reached the bottom, they found row after row of oversized lockers with clear front panels so that they could all see inside. At the front and back of every row was a cart. Not a shopping cart, but a long, wide wooden platform on wheels.

Sensei Chow divided them into two teams. Team one was on first response and members of team two were given bedrolls so that they could sleep for three hours. Team one would be on patrol until midnight, then they'd get to rest for three hours while team two took the lead.

Steve, Sam, Darcy, and Nora were on team one.

"I need four ninjas at each end of each row," Sensei Chow instructed. "You'll quickly figure out what items are in your row."

Darcy fell in with Steve and Sam and Nora. They had to occupy the very last row.

The lockers in their aisle were filled with things on wheels. The skateboards were easy to recognize, as were the bicycles. When Darcy came across the unicycles, she stopped in pure puzzlement. How would these be necessary for any situation, ever?

In the very center of the aisle, there was a single locker that was empty. Darcy opened it up. For an empty locker, it was impossibly clean, not a speck of dust anywhere. She touched the side walls and then the back wall. The back wall felt different. When she pushed against it, it started to turn.

It was a hidden door.

There was a hallway behind it, short enough that it only took three steps to cross it, and it led to another locker. This one was at least five times wider than the others. Its front panel was solid black. Darcy knocked on it and immediately suspected it was made of ultimite. It reminded her of her fight with General Kadek.

There was no lock, no handle, no way of getting it open. It wouldn't take a trained agent to figure out that something very important was being kept here.

But what was it?

STEVE

"Sam," said Steve. "What is the ambassador policy during a war? Are you allowed to be doing this?"

Sam narrowed his eyes. "Well, we *are* supposed to lock down our residence and flee the country. But I can't see my dad ever doing something like that. We've been in Ninjastoria for years and we're happy here."

Steve let out a sigh of relief. "Good. It makes me feel better knowing that you're around."

Then Steve noticed that Darcy wasn't there.

He looked, spotted the open locker, and poked his head inside.

"Sam," Steve whispered. "Get over here."

The two of them went into the locker and stood beside Darcy. They stared at the black storage locker that was definitely keeping a big secret.

"Marcy, what do you think is in there?" Steve asked.

"Something that no one is supposed to know about, probably," she said.

"Or maybe something that isn't even supposed to exist," said Sam. "Like level four scrolls."

Steve felt it in his bones, then. It *had* to be a collection of level four scrolls, containing instructions for how to perform dangerous, forbidden techniques. What else would need to be locked away in a secret safe?

"We should get back into the aisle before anyone notices that we're gone," said Sam. "I don't want to have to go to ninja court for being where I don't belong a second time."

They left the secret locker behind and returned to their assigned spot. When Sensei Chow saw what row they were stationed in, his big eyebrows furrowed. He moved the four of them and appointed them as the first supply delivery team.

"Sorry," he said, raising his eyebrows, "I forgot that we don't need anything from this aisle."

The student teams waited as patiently as they could. Steve could tell that many of them, like himself, were feeling a wobbling sense of dread. What made it worse was the possibility that any second, a bunch of mecha-moles could burst out from the ground.

"Steve, how will we know what supplies need to go where? I would have figured that people would communicate by cell phone or radio, but I don't see Sensei Chow using either of those," Darcy said.

"Well," Steve said, "our most reliable method of fast, long-distance communication in a war is our network of ninja crows and cats. Look, there's one."

A sleek, purplish-black cat darted down the stairs and made its way to Sensei Chow. The cat leaped onto Sensei Chow's shoulder.

"You handwrite little messages and give them to animals?" Darcy asked Steve. "I'm sorry if this sounds rude, but that is very inefficient. You have phones and computers. They send messages instantly."

"Those can be intercepted. Ninja cats and crows are totally loyal to us. One thing, though: we don't write down any messages."

"Then how could the cats and crows possibly relay any information?" she asked.

Steve pointed at the cat perched on Sensei Chow's shoulder.

"The northern border team is requesting twelve more pairs of extra-large nunchakus," said the cat, in a baritone voice.

DARCY

The cat leaped off of Sensei Chow's shoulder and scampered away. Sensei Chow relayed the supply order and a bunch of students scrambled to get the extra-large nunchakus.

Darcy's jaw dropped. She shook her head.

"I've clearly lost my mind," she said.

"Steve, I don't think she knows," said Sam. "I didn't know the full story until I moved here."

"What story?" Darcy asked.

Steve cleared his throat. "This is one of my favorite bedtime stories from when I was a kid. You see, cats came from the moon thousands of years ago. When they still lived on the moon, many of them drank from the hidden magical fountain at the base of Mount Mee-Wow, and the magical water gave them the ability to talk. Then, one day, here on our world, all of the crows decided to take a vacation to the moon. When they got there, they became friends with the cats, so the cats led them to the fountain and gave them the ability to talk, too."

Darcy nodded. Animal vacations. Sudden friendships. Flying to the moon. Like so many things in Ninjastoria, it seemed too far-fetched to be true, which meant that it was probably completely true.

The students in charge of gathering all of the nunchakus

returned and placed them in a backpack. They flung it to Nora and then Sensei Chow gave them directions.

"Okay, team, stick together and get these to the northern border barracks," Sensei Chow said, addressing Nora. "If you encounter the enemy, do whatever you need to get away and make the delivery."

Nora didn't say anything. She accepted the backpack, four hoverboard coins, and led the way out. Steve was right behind her, trying to keep up.

"Nora?" Steve asked. "Please stop being like this. It's a war. We need to work together."

"Whatever," Nora said, handing them their hoverboard coins so that they could summon their boards.

STEVE

Night had fallen. Steve saw a few crows circling above. A half-moon hung low in the sky.

They passed two other ninja squads as they zoomed toward their destination. Other than that, the streets were clear.

Steve tried asking Sam about his favorite new cell phone game, Vegetable Samurai. The conversation quickly fell apart because they had to keep an eye out for mecha-moles.

"How far is it until the northern border?" Darcy asked him.

"Thirty minutes," Steve said. "Unless Nora knows a shortcut or something."

Nora was ahead of them by a good twenty feet.

"Is she going to be okay?" Samurai Sam asked.

"I honestly don't know," Steve said. "Let's just get this done and maybe she'll snap out of it."

Soon enough, they left the city behind. They zipped through the woods, sticking to some of the main hiking trails. Steve was about to tell Darcy that they were making good time when he saw movement in the trees.

"Nora! Wait!" Steve called.

The entire party came to a halt.

"Look up there," Steve said.

Gathered in the high branches of an old, thick-trunked tree, were three ninjas: his mom, his dad, and President Ninja. It was hard to see President Ninja at first, because he was wearing his camouflage uniform *and* his camouflage moustache.

Without a second thought, Steve flew his hoverboard right over to them. Their conversation, which had been too quiet to hear, came to a complete halt.

"Hello, son," said his dad. "This is a good surprise."

"Hey, honey," said his mom. "You doing okay?"

"For now, yeah," Steve said.

"Hello, Ninja Steve," said President Ninja. "I see that you have joined one of the student supply squads. Thank you for your bravery."

"Thank you, sir. Thank you for letting me and Nora out of jail."

"It was necessary," President Ninja said. "Anyway, I need to work something out with your parents. So if you could —"

"LOOK OUT!" Samurai Sam shouted.

The tree shook, then split in half. Steve's parents ran off the end of the branch and landed silently on the ground. His mom and dad drew their baseball bats. President Ninja landed in another tree. Steve hovered in place.

Three brute mecha-moles clawed their way to the surface. A fourth one came out last. Steve saw the golden claws and knew that it was Prince Eldin. Even though Steve had already seen him once before, he was still caught off-guard by just how tall Eldin was. Like last time, he was wearing his gold helmet, his black and gold boots, and his golden chest plate armor. Once again, his weapon of choice was a long stick with a drill bit on each end.

"The ninja with no honor," said Eldin, looking at Steve. "Elom, you may have your revenge tonight."

Steve looked around for the young prince. He spotted him hiding behind one of the other brute mecha-moles. Elom was carrying the same weapon as his father. He stepped into view and stumbled, dropping his weapon.

"Here we go again," mumbled Steve.

"Halt, ninja peasant!" said Elom. "We're going to win this war and shut down your holidays where you dress your prisoners up like mecha-moles and beat them with drumsticks."

There was no holiday like that. Not at all. That didn't even sound fun to Steve. What other lies had Elom been told about Ninjastoria and its people?

"I don't want to fight your son," said Steve.

Prince Eldin roared. "A rat doesn't decide if a raven can eat it! Elom, destroy him!"

The young prince threw his drill spear. It didn't even come

close to reaching Steve.

"Your son isn't a good fighter," Steve told Eldin.

"Steve! Move!" Nora shouted.

Prince Eldin threw *his* drill spear right at Steve. There was a *clang* as Steve's mom threw a shuriken and knocked it off-course. The drill spear tumbled down and stuck in the dirt.

"Big mistake," Steve's mom said.

The mecha-mole erupted. "Your worm of a child has insulted my royal heir."

Steve hovered away until he was with his mom. She was gripping another shuriken and had a pepper-powder bomb ready to throw.

"Take care of the mission," said President Ninja, hopping down from the tree and walking right for Eldin. His posture was rigid, and even though Eldin was way taller than President Ninja, the two of them seemed equal.

"But, sir, we can't leave you on your own," Steve's dad said.

"Shut up," said President Ninja. "I fought all kinds of mecha-moles the last time around. While Raheem was fighting the Mole Emperor, I was keeping the royal guard at bay, including Eldin. I can handle these four, no problem."

Eldin shrugged. "I've become stronger. You've become an old man."

President Ninja clapped his hands. "You're wrong, Eldin. In the meantime, my soldiers have orders to follow."

"Yes, sir," said Steve's mom.

President Ninja said, "It was meant to be an operation for the two of you. But now I realize that it would be better if all of you went together."

"No one's leaving," said Eldin, and that was the signal for an attack.

The mecha-mole closest to Steve and his mom dug into the ground and popped up to the left of Steve's mom. She took the pepper-powder bomb and shoved it right into the mecha-mole's mouth. The powder bomb burst, Steve shot back on his hoverboard, and his mom cleared out before the cloud of burning dust could touch her.

"Follow me!" Steve's mom said. "Your father knows where to meet us."

Steve listened, but he said, "What about Nora and Marcy and Sam?"

He looked back over his shoulder. Sam used his earth-shake magic to throw a mecha-mole off balance, Darcy jump-kicked it in the chest, and Nora used the spell of eight sneezes. They ran off in the opposite direction, with Steve's dad bringing up the rear.

The last thing Steve saw was the squad of mecha-moles surrounding President Ninja.

Steve's mom summoned her own hoverboard and once she and Steve had zoomed off, she made a bird call. A crow dipped down from above and perched on her shoulder.

"President Ninja is fighting Prince Eldin and three brute mecha-moles. Send backup immediately."

The crow squawked and took flight.

"Mom, is President Ninja going to be okay?" Steve asked. Lately, Steve hadn't exactly been the president's biggest fan, what with the jail sentence and all. That being said, even at his angriest, Steve would never have wished for President Ninja to get smacked around by four mecha-moles.

"The president is a tremendous warrior," Steve's mom said. "You should be worried about those poor mecha-moles, not him."

Steve nodded. That was a good point. You couldn't be the president unless you were a supremely talented ninja. After all, you needed enough people in Ninjastoria to believe that you could run the village *and* protect it, if needed.

"I'm glad you're here, Mom," Steve said.

She hovered closer and put an arm around him. "Your father and I, your teachers, every adult in Ninjastoria is going to do everything possible to end this as soon as we can and get everyone's lives back to normal."

Steve let out a big breath. "Yeah."

"Let's go meet up with your father. He and I always have meeting places for times like this. We have a critical mission to complete and you've been assigned to join us."

They met up twenty minutes later at an old windmill in a field of pink potatoes.

His dad hugged him. "Good work back there, big guy."

Steve was about to tell him not to say embarrassing things like that, when a crow flew down and landed on Steve's shoulder.

"Tell Sam that he's in trouble," the crow said, before taking to wing once again.

"What's the mission?" Nora asked, not wondering at all what the crow had talked about. She was no longer carrying the backpack full of nunchakus, so they must have found a way to deliver them, after all.

"I still don't know if we should be taking you," Steve's dad said, and Nora frowned.

"It was an order from President Ninja," said Steve's mom. "I'd prefer to follow it."

"Fine. The mission is a secret visit to —"

Steve's dad stopped.

There was a whooshing of a hoverboard, followed by a clanking of armor as someone approached.

It was Samurai Sam's dad.

DARCY

Although Darcy's time at the bureau had taught her the names and faces of many important political figures, the samurai ambassador to Ninjastoria had not been one of them.

Samurai Sam's dad wore dark blue armor that seemed to absorb the moonlight. His shoulder pads had small spikes, and his helmet was carved to resemble an armadillo's head — the most revered animal in Bushido Gardens. There was a sword in a sheath on each of his hips. He spoke with a crisp voice and his face was stoic.

"Son, you ran away from home during a time of war. I had to enlist the help of the ninjas and their crows in order to track you down. You've dishonored both me and your mother. You know that we are leaving Ninjastoria," he said.

Darcy watched as Sam lowered his gaze to his boots. She could tell, right away, that Sam was used to obeying orders.

"What do you mean?" Ninja Steve asked. "You can't make him leave."

Samurai Sam's dad crossed his arms. "Unlike your parents, Ninja Steve, I've taught my son some discipline."

Darcy couldn't believe that he would throw an insult like that when Ninja Steve's parents were right there. It was not especially fitting behavior for an ambassador to another country.

"I don't appreciate that comment about our parenting, Karl," said Ninja Steve's mom. "That was uncalled for."

"It doesn't matter right now," he said. "My orders are to get out of this place until the war is done. That means my son is coming with me and my wife."

Darcy saw the sadness hit Ninja Steve.

"But this has been your home for years," said Ninja Steve. "You're going to leave it? Just like that?"

"This has been our *post*, Ninja Steve," said Sam's dad. "Our *home* is in Bushido Gardens. So you can say 'goodbye' and then we are gone. Just like that."

Darcy wondered if the samurai ambassador kept his heart encased in armor, too.

"I'm sorry, Steve," said Sam. "This dumb war is ruining everything. I knew we were leaving, so I ran to the school so that I could spend some more time with you and Arjun and Marcy."

"I'm glad you did it," said Steve. "Don't worry. We're going to win this war so fast. We're going to stop those moles and then you can come right back here. Got it?"

"You got it," said Sam.

Steve gave Samurai Sam a crushing hug.

"We need to leave, Sam," said Sam's dad. "Our secret transport is waiting. Your mother's already there."

Sam waved goodbye to everyone as he and his dad hoverboarded away.

"I've always wondered how Sam turned out to be so nice," said Steve's dad. "Karl's a real sword in the mud."

"Don't talk like that," said Steve's mom. "Yes, he's stern. And rude. And I don't like him. You know what, never mind, he *is* a sword in the mud."

"Let's go," said Ninja Steve. His fists were clenched and his posture was rigid. It was, to Darcy, a disquieting sight.

"Only if you're ready, Steve," his dad said. "You want to say anything first? Talk it out, maybe?"

"Yeah, Steve, that was messed up," Nora said.

Darcy didn't say anything. This was what a family could do. She felt, then, a small crystal of ice in her chest. It was awful, she told herself, to feel jealous at a moment like this. But it was true. Darcy could have mentors and teachers and peers. There was a chance, though, that she would never have a family again.

"I want to get going," said Steve. "Whatever this mission is, let's get it done so we can get back here and end the war. Then Sam can come back."

Steve's parents didn't press anymore. They activated their hoverboards. Steve's mom took the lead and his dad was the rear guard. That put Darcy in the middle with Nora and Steve.

As she glided along, Darcy knew what she needed to say, yet she struggled to say it. What good would it do to say, "I'm sorry," to Steve? What would those two words mean, when Steve had said goodbye to his best friend?

She finally dug up the courage to say it. Darcy hovered a little closer, and the words were on her lips when she saw that Steve had tears running down his face. He was trying hard to look straight ahead and to look serious.

He sniffled and wiped his face.

"I'm embarrassed," he said. "I'm sorry."

"You have nothing to be embarrassed about and you have nothing to be sorry about. Today is a terrible day," she said.

"Yes."

"You're going to get through it. *We're* going to get through it," she said, surprising herself with how much she sounded like Lead Agent Evelyn. Or was it Ninja Gertie?

"Thank you," Steve said.

The trip was silent after that. Darcy got more and more anxious as they got closer to the border wall. The faint shapes of black-uniformed ninjas were darting around atop the wall. Every now and then, she'd catch a glimpse of a feline silhouette or a swooping crow.

Steve's mother signaled for everyone to halt. The night was

quiet, and aside from the whoosh of their hoverboards, Darcy never would have guessed that the country was at war.

"We need to talk about this mission," said Steve's mom. "President Ninja has given us a vital task. It's something that will alter the course of this war, so everyone listen up."

Darcy noticed that Nora's mood had significantly improved. She was eager to hear the details with an enthusiasm that normally only Steve would muster.

"This is highly classified information, so there's no written document. Our mission only exists because President Ninja told us. There will be no backup, and there won't be a second chance if we fail," Steve's mom continued. "We have reason to believe that the mecha-moles are close to opening the Nexus."

That word again.

Darcy said, "What is it? No one will tell me."

Steve's mom cleared her throat. "It's another dimensional realm. The Nexus is on the other side of a portal. It is…not a nice place."

"Why would anyone want to open it up, then?" Steve asked.

"Steve, you know that Sensei Raheem defeated the Mole Emperor all those years ago, right?" his dad said.

"Of course. That's why he's a hero," Steve said.

"The Mole Emperor had grown so powerful that no one could

defeat him the normal way. We had to open up a portal to the Nexus and seal him in there."

"This is for real?" Nora asked.

"Yes, sweetie," her dad said. "You need to collect a few enchanted objects in order to open up the portal. President Ninja has learned that the mecha-moles might need only one more object before they can open it up and bring back the Mole Emperor."

A heavy silence fell on all of them. Darcy was having a hard time believing what she had heard. A world that you could enter through a portal? How could that have been kept a secret all this time? It seemed like a thing that should only exist in one of her *Allison the Darkwalker* novels.

"Exactly how many enchanted items do you need to open the Nexus?" Nora asked. "I hope it's not some clichéd number like four."

Darcy knew what Nora was talking about. People loved writing stories that always relied on the number four. Goldenlocks and the *Four* Bears. The *Four* Little Pigs. A lot of stories had magical wish-granting creatures that allowed for *four* wishes. Four was, indeed, an overused number.

"Three," said Steve's dad. "So, no, it's definitely not a storybook cliché."

"What is our actual mission?" Darcy asked.

"We know that the moles already have one Nexus key. Our mission is to ascertain whether or not the moles have gained possession of a second Nexus key, and if so, we are to find a way to take it back."

Darcy bit her lower lip. "Can you tell us what the object is?"

It was an incredibly important detail and yet Steve's parents were being very careful not to say what it was. Was it some kind of weapon? A dangerous animal?

"The Nexus keys are random," said Steve's dad. "The last time we gathered them, we had a pearl from the bottom of the Bottomless Sea, a painting of a walrus, and a bicycle helmet. Once we used them, they lost their powers, and three new objects gained them."

From a mission intelligence standpoint, this was a disaster. They were looking for something...and that special something could actually be anything. Surely, there had to be some pattern or some way to trace a magic signal.

"How did you ever manage to find the three objects in the first place?" Nora asked, stealing Darcy's question.

"That was the bureau's job," said Steve's dad. "Whatever technology they developed, we asked them not to share it with anyone, not even us. The fewer people who could find the Nexus objects, the better."

That didn't make things any easier for them at the moment, though. The mission still sounded impossible.

"What is our destination?" Darcy asked.

Everyone was all ears.

"We must go into mole-controlled territory," said Ninja Steve's mom. "We need to get into the Bureau of Sneakery."

STEVE

"Wow! We get to go to the Bureau of Sneakery," said Steve. "Why would the moles be keeping a Nexus object there?"

Steve's dad said, "The bureau had one. Since the moles have taken the campus, however, no one has been able to get in touch with anyone from the bureau. President Ninja said he couldn't wait any longer, so we are going in to see if we can confirm if the moles have found the object. Also —"

There was a lot of shouting from the ninjas up on top of the wall. Everyone turned to see what was happening. Three mecha-moles were on rocket-powered gliders; not even the best ninja archers could reach them.

"On four," Steve's mom said. "One."

"Two," said Steve's dad, who performed the spell of one puffy cloud.

"Three," said Steve's mom, who performed the spell of cloud-angering.

"Four!" said Nora, who performed the spell of the tiny tornado.

The mini tornado fell from the sky like a spinning top, and it whirled the mecha-moles around before tossing them away from the wall. The last time Steve had seen that technique had been during a professional bowling match. It hadn't ended well.

"Let's move," said Steve's mom. "Details later."

Steve's parents zoomed ahead, keeping close to the ground. When they got to the wall, Steve's dad got off of his hoverboard and head-butted the wall. Part of the ground let out a *hiss* and slid aside to reveal what appeared to be a hidden elevator.

"That was awesome," said Steve. "You have to head-butt the wall to access the secret passage? No one would ever think to do that."

"It's actually an eyeball scanner hidden in the wall. I do the head-butt to impress people," his dad said.

The gel-grips of the hoverboard surfaces released their feet. One by one, they all went into the elevator. The secret opening was covered once more.

There was a one clear, square tile beneath their feet. There were four metal walls and a metal ceiling. When they were all standing on the tile, there was a noise like crickets chirping.

"Wait a minute," said Darcy. "How did you get this?"

"President Ninja worked out a deal," said Steve's mom.

Steve was trying to figure out what was so special about this room that sort of looked like an elevator.

"Okay, we are going to use this to get close to one of the bureau's secret entry points," said Steve's dad, pushing a round, yellow button that caused a touchscreen to appear. He punched in a few numbers and letters.

Beams of blue light came out from the tile's edges and their feet became locked in place. The entire elevator rotated to the right, and Steve could have sworn he was looking at a beach. It rotated left and suddenly he was looking at a room full of wheels of cheese. It rotated left again, and he saw an exploding volcano on a faraway island. The elevator spun in a full rotation and then opened up.

They were face to face with a full squad of scout mecha-moles on guard duty. So much for a secret entry point.

"I bet I can take out more of them than you can, Jackson," said Steve's mom to Steve's dad, immediately jump-kicking a scout mecha-mole out of the way.

"Fine! If I win, we're getting tickets to the Rude Wig Van Beef Oven concert," he said, landing a heel kick square on the butt of a scout mecha-mole.

"Sure thing, honey. I'll suffer through that awful classical heavy metal music if you win. But if *I* win, we're going to see Shallow Shadow rap like you've never heard her before," said Steve's mom, squaring off against another mecha-mole.

Steve was too interested in his parents' conversation. He forgot that he was supposed to be fighting.

He watched as his mom threw a right punch forward and a

left kick backward at the same time, keeping perfect balance like it was a dance move. Two scouts went down.

"Incoming mail!" said Steve's dad, rolling back and flinging a mecha-mole into the air with his foot. Steve's mom snatched it out of the air by its feet, spun, and launched it far past all of the others.

"That one counts as mine," Steve's mom said.

"No way!"

Steve looked over and saw Darcy smiling a faint smile. It was the kind of pure, simple smile that plays on your face when you've forgotten that other people might be looking at you. It was also the kind of smile that made Steve's heart beat a little faster.

The sounds of fighting subsided. Steve's parents walked back into the elevator. They both claimed to have dealt with eight mecha-moles each. An even tie.

"We didn't discuss what would happen if we tied," said his mom. "Let's do both concerts, then."

Steve's dad laughed. "Like, you mean, you want to go on a *date*...with *me*?"

"You are ridiculous," said Steve's mom, laughing.

"This is so embarrassing that I could die right here," said Nora, under her breath.

"Back to serious business," said Steve's dad. "We need to find another way in. This one has been discovered. Maybe there's someone here who knows more about emergency exit routes?"

Steve, like everyone else, turned to look at Darcy.

"I know of one," she said. "But you're probably not going to like it."

DARCY

The Bureau of Sneakery held its fair share of secrets. They included secret classrooms, secret training grounds, secret cafés, and secret passages. The secret cafés were a point of pride for the older students, although some of the younger students believed it was all made up for the sole purpose of making them jealous.

An agent needed to be able to make someone feel like it was okay to reveal a secret, therefore Darcy had to learn some tricks from Evelyn. One of her successes had been in getting Evelyn to talk about the network of access passages to and from the bureau.

It had happened during one of her hacking lessons. Darcy had compared it to traveling through a mountain in order to get to the other side. Evelyn said that it was a fair comparison, because she had done something like that once.

"Why would you ever have the need to travel through a mountain?" Darcy had asked her.

"I was tasked with evaluating one of the lesser-used secret paths as one of my final graduation assessments. A river runs through one of the nearby mountain systems. We built a path alongside it."

Darcy had learned where the mountain was. She had a good idea of where the entrance would be. She also knew that revealing it to the ninjas would be breaking one of the most basic rules of being agent.

If she wasn't an agent anymore, then maybe the penalty wouldn't apply. At the same time, the echo of Commander Natalya's words rang in her mind: "Your watch has been disabled, your boot features have been locked, and you may not set foot on any of our grounds — the girls' or the boys' campus — *ever* again. If you reveal any of our information or attempt to contact anyone in the agency, we will dispatch someone to capture you and lock you away."

She decided it was worth the risk.

"If we set the coordinates for 34.R.1U4, that will get us close to the entrance," she said, remembering what Evelyn had told her.

Steve's parents entered the coordinates and the elevator began to hum. Then, a spark shot out of the control panel. The machine rotated once and made a thunderous *clank*. Darcy looked ahead and saw her old bedroom at the bureau being devoured by flames.

The sight made her feel like someone had squeezed the air out of her lungs. That glimpse of her bed, her cramped closet, and her desk unlocked a homesickness that almost knocked her off her feet. That all of it was aflame made it even worse.

The elevator started spinning like a top, throwing everyone

around. Darcy caught a glimpse of a sand-filled pit; snakes were crawling through it.

"Something's not right," said Steve.

"Good one, Ninja Obvious," said Nora, who was flung against the ceiling as the elevator did a barrel roll.

Darcy saw a whirling mass of visions: a room containing boxes of breakfast cereal stacked from floor to ceiling, a submarine cutting through emerald waters, a vast blackness filled with orange and purple stars.

The elevator came to a halt. The control panel started smoking. The doors parted, but barely.

Darcy pushed the doors apart and held them open. Everyone else squeaked through. She caught a big lungful of bitter smoke and nearly fell over, coughing.

When she could breathe again, she was able to figure out where they were. Luckily, the elevator hadn't dropped them off in the middle of the Scorched Sands or a remote island in the Blackstar Sea.

They were standing in front of a mine.

"This is the right place," said Darcy.

But the sun was out. When they had left Ninjastoria, it had been early in the night.

"How is it daytime already?" Steve asked. "Did it take us that many hours to travel by elevator?"

Nora got out her phone and switched it off of stealth mode so that she could check the time. Her hands started to shake as she shared her discovery.

"It wasn't just hours," she said, turning the phone around for everyone to see. "It's...it's been a full week."

STEVE

Steve couldn't believe his ears. How could a week have already passed? What kind of elevator had they stepped into?

Steve's parents looked alarmed, too.

"The transporter moves instantly through time and space," said Steve's mom. "When it malfunctioned, it must have moved us forward in time."

Steve stopped thinking about their problem, because an even bigger thought popped into his head. "You mean that we have time machines?!"

"No," said Steve's dad. "The technology is only stable for moving from place to place, not time to time. When it was being developed, any attempt to purposely move forward or backward in time made the machine explode. We're very lucky to be alive."

"Nora, we aren't a thousand years in the future, are we?" asked Darcy.

"No. The display still says the same year. Just seven days later. What if…what if we've lost the war?" Nora asked.

That thought hadn't yet occurred to Steve. It was entirely possible that Ninjastoria could have surrendered.

Steve texted Arjun immediately. "How's the war?"

Arjun replied, "Very loud. The moles haven't won any big

victories yet, but neither have we. Where have you been all week?"

Steve texted, "Delivering supplies. It's complicated. Be safe."

A wave of exhaustion passed over Steve. Maybe it was from all of the tension from the start of the war. Maybe it was from being hurled seven days into the future. He looked around and it seemed like everyone was feeling the same way.

"We need to sleep," said Steve's dad. "Might as well lie down right here."

The ground was rocky, but Steve was able to sleep. His mom woke him and the others at noon.

Steve examined the sign on the mine that read "Mine Your Own Business!" It looked like no one had set foot in the place for years.

"I have good news and I have bad news about this mine," said Darcy.

The ninjas looked at her.

"The good news is that we can still get to the bureau if we travel through it," she said.

Then, she paused.

"What's the bad news?" Steve asked.

"The mine was sealed off because it had become a nesting ground for bear-wolves."

Steve noticed that Nora had gone pale. He figured it was from all of the spinning in the elevator. Or was it possible that his fearless sister was actually scared of something?

Nora asked, "Is there another route?"

Darcy touched her fingers to her chin and thought for a moment. "Even with our hoverboards, it would take at least a full day of traveling to find another access point. With the elevator broken, this is the only way to get to the bureau quickly."

"There's...there's no other way?" Nora tried again.

"No," said Darcy.

Steve's parents nodded as they stared down the entrance. A strand of rail tracks for a mine cart ran out of the mine, like a tongue sticking out of a mouth. The entrance itself was maybe ten feet high, fifteen feet wide. The walls were jagged, exposed rock, dotted with disks that glowed with a soft, blue light. Some of them were cracked, some of them were flickering like spark-bugs.

"At the very least, bear-wolves can't transform unless they're exposed to moonlight," Steve said.

"Weird. You don't normally remember these kinds of things," Nora said.

"Well, one time, right after an episode of Kung-Food, there

was a show where pairs of bear-wolf trackers were chasing down bear-wolves in order to win a prize. I was too lazy to look for other shows, so I watched the whole thing," Steve said.

He remembered the trackers talking about the effect of moonlight, how it would turn a fearsome wolf into a fearsome bear.

The show also had occasional interviews with biologists, most of whom weren't quite sure why the bear-wolf had evolved the way it had. After all, there didn't seem to be any distinct advantage to transforming into a bear when the animal was already a skilled, fearsome hunter as a wolf.

Darcy carefully led the way on her hoverboard beside the rail tracks. Steve was half a pace behind her. There was no sign of a mine cart anywhere.

"I guess this is as good of a hidden entrance as any," Steve said. "How long do you think it will take to get there?"

"A few hours, I think," said Darcy.

"Are you nervous about this?" he asked.

"I am," she said. "I don't know what we're going to find when we get there. That's what scares me the most."

"It's going to be fine. We're all here with you, remember?" he said.

"But what if the mecha-moles ruined everything? What if the

entire campus is in flames? Or what if my superiors are there and they see me and immediately imprison me for coming back?" she asked.

"Forget those," Steve said. "What if you can help reclaim the place? What if you can find out something that the mecha-moles don't want anyone to know? What if you do a really cool jump kick?"

"Those are much better 'what if' questions," Darcy said. "I like the way you think."

The mine cart path split then, one path going straight ahead and the other taking a sharp right. Darcy went right and everyone followed.

There was a howl.

A long, high-pitched howl.

A howl that echoed all the way down the mineshaft.

"Bear-wolf," muttered Steve. "I wonder if we'll cross paths with it."

Darcy turned another corner and came to a screeching halt. She threw her hand to the side and caught Steve, nearly clotheslining him. The gel grip of the board kept it from flying out from under his feet.

Standing in the middle of the tracks was a bear-wolf in wolf form. Its coat was mostly silver, although there was a fine layer of brown dust on it from being in the mine. The beast was as tall as Steve and just as wide. It was unnaturally slender, standing on limber legs that ended in three-toed claws. It had a black nose and yellow eyes that seemed to flicker. Like all bear-wolves, it had no tail, and like all bear-wolves, its mouth had two rows of sharp, tiny teeth.

"Steve, get away from that," Nora said, her voice quaking. "Please, get back."

Steve and Darcy began to inch their hoverboards backward. The wolf took small steps forward, sniffing the air and then pawing at it.

Then, it sat down on its hind legs, pulled its head back, and let out a piercing howl.

"I'm out of here," Nora said, and Steve looked back just in time to see her turn and head back in the direction of the entrance. Steve's mom went after her.

A few more howls came from deeper in the mine. One by one, more wolves began to slink through the corridor. Their steps were impossibly smooth; they looked like silvery shadows sliding across the ground. Steve wondered if the ninjas could learn a thing or two by studying the way they moved.

Steve and Darcy were with Steve's father, about ten feet between them and the animals. The other wolves sat behind the leader, forming a pyramid: one wolf, two wolves, three wolves.

"This is odd," said Steve's dad.

The wolf in front stood up, pawed at the ground. The others parted to the sides and let their leader through. Now Steve thought the wolves were all looking directly at *him*.

"I think they want us to follow," Steve said.

"That's a big assumption," said Darcy.

"Yeah, Steve, they eat people like us for breakfast. Or lunch, or dinner," said his dad.

One of the remaining wolves gave a timid whine. The others did the same. They began to slink away, one by one. Steve thought it looked like the saddest parade.

"Marcy, do we need to follow this path?" Steve's dad asked.

"Yes, this is the way," she said.

"Fine. I'm going first. Let's stay on our boards in case we need to make a break for it," said Steve's dad.

Steve and Darcy drifted along behind his dad. He wondered what it was about the bear-wolves that frightened Nora so much. They seemed very ninja-like: soft-stepping, respectful, and team-oriented.

When they finally caught up with the bear-wolves, they were all pacing back and forth in front of a pile of boulders and rocks, letting out little whimpers. The pile was blocking off a side-route from the mineshaft, and Steve thought he could hear the calls of more wolves from the other side.

Steve saw the scratch marks on the boulders and realized that the bear-wolves had been pawing at them, but there was nothing they could do to move them.

"This seems easy enough, Dad," Steve said.

Just then, Nora and Steve's mom returned. Nora stayed far, far away, her hoverboard darting back and forth. Steve's dad explained the situation to Steve's mom.

"I wish we had a samurai here with us," said Steve's mom. "One of their earth-shake spells could turn all of these rocks into mud in an instant. Instead, I guess we'll have to use the spell of rock and roll."

Steve watched as his dad crossed his arms over his chest and then swung one arm around in a sweeping circle, like the second hand of a clock. His mom did the same. Then, they did some quick stepping and touched their knuckles against the rocks. The boulders at the top began to tremble, then roll back and forth, slowly working themselves free. One by one, they rolled down and hit the other side of the mineshaft.

When the top half of pathway was opened, the bear-wolves darted through.

"Wow, you should check this out," said Steve's dad.

They all peeked over the boulder barricade.

There was a litter of fuzzy, gray-brown bear-wolf cubs, ten of them. They were running in between the legs of the adults, barking with excitement.

"See? I told you they wanted us to follow them," Steve said. "Now they're back with their cubs. Nora, there's really nothing to be afraid of."

"That's a foolish thing to say," came a voice from farther down the tunnel. "There's plenty to be afraid of down here."

DARCY

Darcy knew that voice and she was sick of it. "Come out, Three. There's no point in being so dramatic."

The man in the gray mask shrugged as he appeared.

Darcy felt the ghost fire building up in her fingertips. She couldn't find a good reason for it, though. None of her meetings with Three had ever led to a fight. So why was there this instinct that told her she was in terrible danger?

Then, she saw that Steve's parents had their weapons out, too.

"I've been to the bureau. You're not going to like it very much when you see it," Three said.

Darcy immediately pictured her dorm building with its windows punched out and smoke pouring through. She imagined her bed and her desk burning down into black ash.

"Get out of here, Hiro," Steve's dad said to Three.

Hiro? That was such an ordinary name.

"I'm only here to help," Three said.

"Yeah, just like you helped Vanessa," Steve's dad said. "You ruined her and her family."

Darcy began to wonder what kind of shared history these two men had. She wondered if any of it might explain why he kept appearing to speak to her.

Three pointed at Darcy. "Don't forget what I told you last

time."

The memory was clear. He'd told her to hack into her own file at the bureau. But now she wondered if he had gotten there first and tampered with it. Would she be playing directly into some plan of his?

Then he pointed at Nora. "When you're tired of being held back, I'll find the right teacher for you. It's a shame to see someone so talented get treated so—"

"That's enough, Hiro," said Steve's mom. "Leave."

He pulled back the long sleeve of his overcoat and revealed his watch. Soon enough, the usual river of glowing ones and zeroes spilled out of it and formed a portal on the ground. Three stepped into it and was gone.

This time, Darcy was close enough to get a good glimpse of the watch face. The display was nearly identical to all of those given out by the Bureau of Sneakery. Had Three once been an agent?

"You called him 'Hiro,'" said Darcy.

"When he was in elementary ninja school, the other kids used to call him 'Zero,'" said Steve's mom.

Darcy was careful about her next words. This was an opportunity she didn't want to lose.

She said, "He's a ninja, then."

Steve's parents looked at each other.

"Well," said Steve's dad, "he *was* a ninja."

As they continued on their hoverboards, the only sound that broke the silence was the occasional drip of water from somewhere ahead of them.

It was Nora who spoke next. "I fought him, Mom. He's not a ninja."

"You *what?!* When was this?" Steve's mom said.

"It was before I left for Botsylvania. He followed me home, wouldn't leave me alone, so I—"

"He got inside the house, Nora used the spell of dragon breath, and he blocked it," Steve said.

Darcy could sense the growing horror from Steve's parents. Their posture went rigid and their fingers curled into fists. She didn't have to see their eyes to know what they were feeling.

"I will keep this short," said Steve's mom. "Hiro came to us from the Bureau of Sneakery. There was something not quite right about him, and the bureau felt that some time in Ninjastoria would help. Instead, he got picked on by the other ninjas. I think it got to him."

Darcy thought of Ninja Steph and Ninja Kelly, the way they were treating her. She knew that if she hadn't been connected with Steve and Sam and Nora and Gertie, there was a chance it would have damaged her severely.

"Hiro went down the wrong path. He took Vanessa with him. He pursued the forbidden level four techniques — the ones that are so powerful that they will eventually drive you mad — but Vanessa was the one who really became addicted. It turned her against us," said Steve's mom.

Darcy bit her lower lip. "Vanessa?"

Steve's dad answered. "President Ninja's sister."

STEVE

Steve recalled his breakfast with President Ninja. The president had spoken about Vanessa then, how she was talented like Nora, how her talent had overshadowed his.

There was more to the story, though, than he had realized. There was a twist, a break in the family tree.

"Where is President Ninja's sister these days?" asked Steve as they continued to walk through the mine.

"We don't know," said Steve's mom.

There was a dip in the mineshaft and then a serpentine curve. Steve noticed a glimmering line running along the wall, like a strand of a spider's web. This one was neon orange. Eventually, it crossed paths with a swirling strand of yellow. There were more and more of the colorful strands, some jagged, some gentle.

There were so many of them that the mineshaft began to glow with multicolored light.

"Whoa," said Steve. "What is this?"

"Bivvite," said Darcy and Nora at the same time.

"It's named after the guy who discovered it, Roy G. Biv," Nora added.

"What can you do with it?" Steve asked.

"You turn it into ink or paint," said Darcy.

The glowing streaks of light thinned out and faded.

"Stop here," said Darcy.

There was a single lantern hanging from a spike on the wall. Darcy pressed on the spike. A mine cart came wheeling toward them.

Painted on its side were the words, "Mario's Carts."

Steve's dad looked at it and said, "I remember seeing commercials for these. That Mario guy really loved two things: carts and mushrooms."

"The cart is a decoy, but pushing the spike unlocks something farther down the path," said Darcy. "Follow me."

Steve watched as she walked straight through the wall.

He stood right in front of it. When he touched his hand against it, it felt solid. But when he pressed harder, it gave way. The texture reminded Steve of wet sand.

Darcy had gotten off of her hoverboard. She was standing in front of a mirror. Her face was smudged with dust, as were all of theirs, but Steve thought that Darcy wore it better than any of them.

The mirror filled with dark blue text, lines of ones and zeroes. Darcy pressed her thumb against it and held it there.

"UNRECOGNIZED."

She frowned and pressed again.

"UNRECOGNIZED."

"They really did wipe me out of the system," said Darcy, her voice breaking. "I'm sorry."

Steve's mom put a hand on her shoulder. "They made a terrible mistake."

Then, Steve's mom pulled off her black glove and pressed her thumb against the mirror. The blue text flashed white.

"RECOGNIZED."

The mirror turned sideways, revealing a walkway that continued on. Steve saw Darcy's face scrunch up in confusion, so he asked the question that he knew both of them were thinking about.

"Mom," said Steve. "Is there something you need to tell us?"

"No," said his mother. "Marcy, please lead the way."

The moment they went past the mirror, their hoverboards shut down.

Steve had just picked his up when the floor dropped out from underneath them.

DARCY

One moment she was picking up a hoverboard. The next moment she was plummeting fifty feet toward a pit full of emergency landing gel.

Darcy did the landing trick that Ninja Steve had taught her. When she hit, instead of breaking through the surface of the blue-green gel, she landed as softly as a shadow. The ninjas had all done the same.

She tried reactivating her hoverboard. It was no use. All of the boards had stopped responding.

"We'll have to find a different way out of the bureau," said Nora, leaving her board behind with everyone else's.

By the edge of the gel pit, there was a single purple button. Darcy pressed it and the rock wall split apart, revealing a long dirt ramp leading up and away from the gel pit.

They all followed her up the ramp until they came to a set of stairs. At the top was a metal hatch that Darcy popped open.

She poked her head out and she breathed a sigh of relief when she heard crashing waves. They were somewhere inside of the coastal mission simulation zone, far from the center of campus.

She looked back. "It's clear."

Darcy hadn't been to the coastal mission simulation zone since she was ten. The ocean section of it went out for four hundred yards, with a coastline that was three hundred yards long. Her practice mission had been to approach on kayak, hide the kayak in the dunes, and search the area to find a defendable observation point for monitoring the water.

This time she wanted to find an observation point that looked toward campus, not toward the water.

"We're near the main campus," Darcy said. "With hoverboards, we could get there in twenty five minutes. Where exactly are we supposed to go?"

"President Ninja's information said that the most likely place to check would be The Giga Squad's lab," said Ninja Steve's mom.

Darcy nodded. "That's near the edge of this zone."

"Since it's full of agent technology, our best bet is to consider it fully guarded and occupied," said Steve's dad. "Especially if it turns out they're keeping Nexus keys there."

Darcy nodded, but she wasn't listening. She was feeling the sand beneath her boots and hearing the waves lapping against the shore. It took her back to when she was an agent, when she felt safe on campus, when she felt like she knew where her life was going. She was going to become the best agent and she was going to find her parents.

She touched her wrist where her watch should have been. In

her head, she was headed back to her dorm, where she could shower, change into a fresh uniform, and see Matilda in the café. Later, she'd have a lesson with Evelyn, and then she'd study until she fell asleep.

"That was the past," Darcy muttered. "The past is gone and this is your life now."

"Hey," said Steve, poking her on the shoulder.

Back to reality. Back to being not-an-agent and not-a-ninja.

"Okay, so let's talk approaches. The Giga Squad lab has four entrances," Darcy said. "Like a plus sign. Those are the only ways in, unless the moles did some tunneling."

"Could we go in through the roof?" Nora asked.

"No. The lab is built with extra thick reinforced concrete and steeltanium, just in case something goes wrong and blows up," Darcy said.

A siren blared. The sky darkened in a matter of seconds. Darcy jumped.

"Oh no," she said.

"What?" asked Steve.

Darcy turned and looked back at the water. A giant wave was rising up. The ninjas saw it, too.

"They know we're here," said Darcy.

They all started running across the sand. Ahead of them was a brush forest: nothing but prickly bushes and low, leafy plants. Steve looked back once and saw that the wave was twenty, maybe thirty feet high and rising.

"Why would that be a part of your training simulator?!" Steve yelled.

"All of our training grounds function as defense, in case someone were to infiltrate the bureau," she said.

"That wave is going to crash before it reaches us," said Steve's mom.

"Then I have just the thing," said Nora.

The wave curled like a closing fist and it pounded the coast. A spray of water shot up like a geyser and there was a roar that reminded Steve of Toran the Tiger. Floodwaters rushed forward, faster than even Hussain Bolt, the greatest ninja sprinter, could have run.

Nora pulled a blue marble out of a hidden pocket. She flicked it ahead of them and there was a puff of smoke. When it cleared, there was an orange rubber raft and two black paddles. They all leaped in.

The waters came surging, kicking the raft forward. The raft took off and Steve fell on his butt. Nora had one paddle, Darcy had the other, and they were rowing furiously.

"We're headed straight for the lab," said Darcy.

So much for a stealthy approach. Steve saw the lab, though it was still distant. True to what Darcy had said, it looked like a plus sign. Steve could also see small dots spreading out. The mecha-moles were preparing for their arrival.

Beyond that, he saw part of the campus. A tall, cone-shaped building that had chunks knocked out of it. A blue metal structure in the shape of a hexagon with shattered windows. All of these were places that Darcy might have known or cared for. All of them had been damaged. He saw the empty expression on her face as she took it all in, and he had no clue how to help her.

"What's the plan?" asked Nora.

"We're going right through the front door," said Steve's mom. "Follow your father's lead. He's an expert in situations like this."

Steve nodded. He felt the weight of the wooden baseball bat slung across his back. He told himself that it was time to hit some homeruns like Hall-of-Famer Babe Ruthless.

The flood began to thin out, though their raft kept zooming onward. There were plenty of scout and brute mecha-moles waiting for them.

Steve watched his dad move to the front of the raft. He held his baseball bat up high.

"We come in peace!" he shouted.

Then, while the raft was still moving, he jumped off of it and planted a heel kick right into a brute mecha-mole's chest. It grunted and went flying back.

"Did I mention that it's opposite day?!" Steve's dad yelled.

Nora shouted that he was so cheesy, but Steve thought that his dad was the coolest. There was no time for talking, though.

Steve went with Darcy, who had drawn her chromega dagger. The mecha-moles sniffed the air.

"Metal!" said one of the brute mecha-moles, holding a big axe. "How careless."

Even though it was nearly twice as big as Darcy, she didn't flinch when it got near. A scout mecha-mole was also targeting Darcy, and Steve slipped away to meet it, head-on.

He ducked the mecha-mole's claw swipe, spun like a top, and used the baseball bat to knock its legs out from under it. Then, Steve swung the bat like a golf club and struck the mecha-mole right on its butt, knocking it out of commission.

He turned just in time to see Darcy's chromega dagger cut the brute mecha-mole's axe in half. The mecha-mole was shocked and let its guard down. Darcy jumped up and punched it in the stomach, then Steve swung his bat and knocked the mehca-mole over.

"Let's go!" said Nora.

She snapped her fingers, made a clicking sound with her tongue, and knelt.

"Cover your eyes!" yelled Steve.

The spell of raging lightning caused a brilliant flash of light. Steve suspected that the mecha-moles, who lived mostly underground, were in a lot of pain from seeing that.

"To the door," said Nora.

Steve's parents were already at the door, which was an intimidating slab of gray metal. His mother, father, and Nora all performed the spell of dragon breath in quick succession, melting a hole right through the middle.

One by one, they all dived through.

Steve ran past door after door. Sometimes there was a big, wide window and he could see black tables, robotic arms, and all kinds of microscopes. There were machines he had never seen: ones with spindly legs, ones with lots of wrenches and screw-drivers, and one that looked like a nacho cheese fountain that was actually running.

Steve was so focused on making it to the next chamber that he didn't notice the mecha-mole that dropped down from the ceiling, right behind him.

He didn't notice until his mom yanked him out of the way

and took the kick instead of him. Then, a black net shot out of the mecha-mole's claw and sealed Steve's mom inside.

"It's been a while," said the mecha-mole, who Steve recognized at once.

DARCY

"Drogar," said Darcy.

Drogar stepped over the net that had pinned down Steve's mom. Like her brother, Prince Eldin, Princess Drogar was twice the height of most ninjas. Darcy saw that Drogar was the shorter of the two royal siblings, maybe eleven feet tall. Her mechanical claws had been enhanced since the last time and now they were a deep, polished green.

"No one picks on my girlfriend and gets away with it," said Steve's dad.

"Isn't she your wife?" said Drogar.

"Yeah, but she's my girlfriend, too," said Steve's dad.

"You're pretty mouthy for a ninja," said Drogar, standing as tall as she could.

Darcy wondered if there was anything she could do to de-escalate the situation. There had been a time when Drogar had been her ally, when they had looked out for each other. Now that there was open war between the mecha-moles and the ninjas, that option was gone.

When she looked around, Darcy noticed that Nora was nowhere to be found. That was a good thing, and the more Darcy could stall for time, the more chances there were that Nora would find the Nexus key.

"You've ruined my home," said Darcy.

Drogar huffed. "It was ours to take."

"That's a lie," said Darcy. "You have no more right to take this place than we would have to take The Mole Republic from you."

Darcy sheathed her chromega dagger. She needed more to say, something that would keep Drogar distracted from the fact that Nora was missing.

"This is about your father, isn't it?" said Darcy.

"Stop pretending that you know anything about me," said Drogar.

Darcy smiled. This was a good sign. Whenever a target insisted that you didn't know her, you were on the right path to making her seriously annoyed.

"I know more about you than you think. I know that you'd really like to fight Sensei Raheem. Yet, for some odd reason, you've been ordered to stay here. Your brother, Prince Eldin, is part of the siege of Ninjastoria," Darcy said. "Is it because you're a princess? Is it because your country values males more than females?"

"No more talking," said Drogar.

The mecha-mole's claws began to hum, and they transformed into wide, flat squares with spikes bristling out of them.

"I don't want to fight you," said Darcy. "None of us do."

"*I* want to," said Steve's dad.

"So do I," said Steve's mom, still struggling in the net.

Darcy clenched her fists. This wasn't going to work. Steve's parents were too worked up, too eager to fight.

Drogar wasn't expecting Steve's dad to take the offensive against her. The moment he was in motion, Steve's mom rolled herself behind Drogar and, despite being stuck in the net, managed to get into a table pose. Steve's dad dodged Drogar's big swing and drove his palms straight into her abdomen. The impact sent her reeling back, and she tripped over Steve's mom.

Without missing a beat, Steve's dad sliced open the net with a throwing dagger, and Steve's mom burst free.

"We've got this," said Steve's mom. "You two know what to do!"

Darcy and Steve took off. Unfortunately, though, she *didn't* really know what to do. They didn't know what the object was or where to start looking. There wasn't even a guarantee that it was in the lab. Really, it might not be anywhere on the campus at all.

"Where do we go next?" Steve asked.

"I've only been in here once," Darcy said. "Let's go down. It would make sense to store the valuable or dangerous stuff there."

She spotted a way down on the left. A mole tunnel led beneath a security gate. She barreled through the tunnel, Steve only two steps behind her. Once they popped out on the other side, they were right near a stairwell.

"I bet there's all kinds of cool gear waiting for us to try it out," said Steve. "Like a remote-control dinosaur that can shoot grenades out of its nostrils. Or maybe a skateboard that has pogo sticks underneath it so that it can jump over stuff."

Darcy didn't have the extra energy to tell him that neither of those existed. It would be difficult to be sneaky if you had a grenade-shooting dinosaur. People would notice you if your skateboard did something that no other skateboard could do.

Upon hitting the bottom of the stairs, there was another security door. This one had been blasted wide open. Straight through it was a lab. Darcy saw the glowing computer screens and she went straight for them.

"Hey, what's going on?" Steve asked.

Darcy only partially heard him. She had booted up the laser keyboard, which was now projecting red letters and numbers into the air in front of her. She hit a series of keystrokes, bypassed the login screen, and started typing up a flurry of complicated command prompts. It was time to hack into her profile and see what Three had been hinting at.

"Fine, I'll stand guard," Steve said, jumping up onto the ceiling.

Darcy didn't want Three to be right. She didn't want to dig into the bureau's files and find out that they had been hiding information from her. Then again, she wasn't sure if she'd be able to even gain access.

It wasn't difficult to bring up a browser and direct herself to the bureau's encrypted data gateway. Evelyn had taught her advanced hacking, but had warned Darcy not to try it on their own systems or else she would risk expulsion for nosing around.

Well, she was already expelled. What was the worst that could happen?

To Steve's credit, he waited patiently and didn't ask any questions. He paced back and forth on the ceiling.

Darcy's fingertips were a blur. Her first attempt failed and set off a security alert. If someone was still monitoring the network from a secure location, he or she was already alerted to Darcy's presence. The second attempt worked.

She pulled up the student registry and found her code number. There were eleven files, each numbered.

Darcy had to hurry. She clicked on file "002." It was a list of her classes from when she was nine. She tried "004." It was a letter of recommendation from Agent Kamala.

It was "009" that she opened next.

It was only one sentence.

But when she read it, she shouted and punched the desk.

STEVE

When Darcy shouted, Steve fell right off of the ceiling. He landed in a crouch.

He heard noises coming from down the hall. They were mechanized noises.

"What's wrong?" he asked.

Darcy shook her head. "I...I..."

Steve walked over. "It's going to be okay."

"No. No, it's not," Darcy said. "How can you even say something like that? Like you know the future?"

Steve put his hands on her shoulders. It made him feel a little dizzy, but he still did it. He looked her right in the eyes.

"It's going to be okay because we are going to make it be okay," he said.

At that moment, two scout mecha-moles spotted them. Steve drew his baseball bat and threw it as they entered the door. The bat caught one of them right on the nose, and the mole flopped onto its back.

Then, before the other could react, Steve had jumped over its head. His feet only touched the ground for a second and then he threw a back-kick that hit its target. Just as Sensei Raheem had taught him, he literally kicked its butt.

"Time to go," Steve said.

He watched Darcy type in a final command. Steve swept up his baseball bat and then they were on the move again.

There was a scratching noise from above. The ceiling opened up, as if someone had taken a bite out of it.

Drogar landed, followed shortly by Steve's parents. All of them looked scratched up, but Drogar was completely out of breath.

"Tell us where the Nexus key is," said Steve's dad.

"Trust us, you don't want to open it, anyway. The place is a nightmare zone," said Steve's mom.

"The second key is here and it belongs to us," said Drogar. "And I am going to get the third one and bring our rightful ruler—my father—back here where he belongs."

Steve clutched his baseball bat. He didn't want to have to fight Drogar. They had worked well together in order to make it through Botsylvania.

"Drogar, he lost his mind and was going to destroy the world," said Ninja Steve. "That is why Sensei Raheem had to stop him. You know that, right?"

"You have the story wrong," said Drogar. "He was going to bring order to the world. He was going to make the moles triumphant, like we deserve. You were the ones who were going to destroy the world if he failed. Somehow, he lost, and The

Mole Republic became a war zone because of you and your wicked ways."

Steve scratched his head. "That is a very different version of things."

"Mine is the only version that matters," said Drogar.

In his heart, Steve sided with his parents. If they told him that the Mole Emperor had gone insane and needed to be banished to the Nexus, he was pretty sure that their version of the story was accurate. After all, they knew what insanity was like, what with him and Nora making all kinds of trouble.

"It's very convenient," said Ninja Steve's dad, "that you blame us for your country becoming a war zone. After all, weren't you the one who declared war on your brother, Eldin, in your battle for the crown? Doesn't some of the blame fall on *your* shoulders?"

Drogar was silent.

"So you're going to open the Nexus?" asked Steve's mom.

"Yes," said Drogar. "We know that you ninjas are holding the final key in Ninjastoria."

As she finished her sentence, a ring of brute mecha-moles dug out of the ground and surrounded them. At first glance, Steve counted ten. But before he could count any higher, another one popped up right next to him, grabbed him by the ankle, and threw him through an open window into a laboratory.

Steve whirled around in the air, made sure that his heels hit the wall, and then he landed on the floor on his feet. His first instinct was to get back out into the brawl. His eyes, however, had spotted something interesting.

In the corner of the laboratory was a table with a green control pad on it. It had two control sticks and two buttons. Standing right next to it was a metallic something covered by a tan sheet.

Steve vaulted over the table and snatched the sheet away. Standing there was a robot dinosaur as big as a brute mecha-mole. Steve knew that it was a scaled down version of Tremendosaurus. That was about the only thing he found interesting when Sensei Raheem taught them about the dinosaur assassins.

The robot was varying shades of green and brown, with metallic feathers sprouting from the backs of its claws and its tail. The eyes were big bulbs and its mouth was wide open, showing rows of metallic teeth.

Steve picked up the remote control. He pressed the big green button with the power symbol. The dinosaur's eye bulbs turned on, a pale yellow.

"This is the greatest day of my life," said Steve.

He tested the control sticks. The dino was on wheels and it

zipped back and forth and side to side. There was only one other button on the control pad. It was a red square. Steve had some idea of what it might do. After all, it was red.

Steve piloted the dino out of the lab and into the hallway. His parents and Darcy were totally surrounded. There was still no sign of Nora.

The mecha-moles all turned and sniffed the air. Metal. The dino was made of metal. Steve realized he didn't have much time before it would be devoured.

Steve pushed the red button.

The dino's mouth opened wide and a single, metallic cylinder shot out. It struck one mecha-mole right in its abdomen, and then the cylinder unfolded into a pair of giant speakers. Colorful lights began beaming out of the dino's chest and then MC Blackbelt's #1 hit rap single, "Roundhouse to the Dome" started blasting from the speakers. The bass notes were so deep that Steve could feel his teeth vibrating.

Mecha-mole after mecha-mole covered its ears. The dino bot began to do some kind of breakdance martial art. Steve watched in awe as it bobbed and swayed around the mecha-moles before using its tail and sweeping their legs out from under them in a whirlwind spin. Many of them were at a disadvantage since they were using their hands to protect their ears.

In a flash, the dancing dino bot had knocked out every mecha-mole except for Drogar.

"You're losing," said Steve.

The Tremendosaurus roared.

And then its battery died.

DARCY

The Giga Squad had once been described to Darcy as a "strange collective of scientists." In her head, she pictured people who never left the lab, who didn't sleep much, who drank a lot of coffee. She hadn't exactly pictured them as people who made dancing dinosaur robots. Plus, she had a hard time imagining Commander Natalya or the Director approving such a project.

Nevertheless, she had been thrilled to watch it thrash all of those mecha-moles. And, she supposed, it was fitting that Ninja Steve had been the one to find it and put it to use. If there was anyone who was meant to control an invention like that, it was Steve.

But most of The Giga Squad's projects never made it to the rest of the bureau—at least, not on the girls' campus. Maybe on the boys' campus or on the adult campus, things were different. Many of the inventions, Darcy figured, were too unpredictable or too costly. Or, like the dinosaur, maybe they had limited battery life.

The speakers stopped blasting music. The flashing lights died out. The dinosaur came to a standstill. Thankfully, it had taken care of most of the mecha-moles, so now the odds were stacked against Drogar.

"We can't let you keep those Nexus keys," said Steve's dad.

"We can't let you open the Nexus, either."

Darcy hated that word. Hated that place. She hated it even more after she had found that email. The one that had —

Drogar turned and ran.

Darcy and the ninjas pursued.

Drogar led them into a room full of glowing orange tubes that ran from floor to ceiling. There were dozens of them. In each one, suspended in the middle of the fluorescent orange liquid, was an object. A bowling ball, a cuckoo clock, a hairbrush, a lightbulb, a ladder. The list went on.

"Is this…?" asked Darcy.

"This is brilliant," said Steve's mom. "The Nexus keys are random every time. With so many objects here like this, an outsider has no idea which one is the actual Nexus key."

Darcy noticed, however, that the moles would have had plenty of time to smash the tubes and take the objects. The fact that they were all still here meant that whatever security feature was in place was a good one.

"We figured out that if we tried to remove any of these without disabling the security set-up first, there would be a chemical reaction that would instantly dissolve every single object," said Drogar.

Then Drogar smashed her enormous fist into one of the tubes.

It cracked. An alarm went off. One by one, the orange tubes turned red. The objects dissolved into confetti-sized particles.

"If we can't have this Nexus key, then no one can. By the time it regenerates, we'll have steamrollered every country with our army, and then we can take our time finding it. I can wait until then." In a flash, she had dug a tunnel up through the ceiling, and was gone.

Everyone breathed a sigh of relief. Everyone except for Darcy. She stared at the red liquid that was eating away at the objects inside. Her throat seized up.

She felt embers licking out from her fingertips.

"This isn't fair," said Darcy.

Ninja Steve and his parents all gave her confused looks. Steve asked what was wrong.

"I lost my opportunity," she said, gesturing at the empty tubes.

"No way," said Steve. "This is a gained opportunity, even if Drogar is still out there. Without the key, the Nexus can't be opened by them anytime soon. Right, Mom?"

"That is correct," said Steve's mom. "The key could regenerate anywhere. It could take years or decades for anyone to find it. This mission isn't a failure."

"Maybe for you it's a success," said Darcy.

She was trying to contain her anger. Deep down, she wished she hadn't hacked into the bureau's systems. She wished she had never read that file. Because now she knew that...

"Marcy, everything is fine. There's a chance that we've scattered their forces and that the bureau can retake the campus," Steve said.

"My parents," said Darcy. Her left hand was totally enveloped in flames. She was losing control of her anger.

"My *parents* are stuck in the *Nexus!*"

STEVE

"Oh," said Ninja Steve.

That was all his brain could come up with. Darcy had just watched her chance at reaching her parents literally disintegrate before her eyes, and all he could say was, "Oh."

He couldn't fully imagine what she was going through. Then again, having part of your body burst into flames seemed like a fairly reasonable response. Steve realized that if his parents had been stuck in some mystery realm for years and then he lost his best chance to reach them, he'd be feeling some fiery anger, too.

Steve and Nora had both seen Darcy's fire power before. He had forgotten that his parents hadn't. They were looking at her with uncertain eyes and she was looking back at them.

Steve's mom spoke. "Marcy, if your parents are still alive, we are going to do everything we can to get them out."

"Will anyone approve that?" Darcy asked.

"Pull it together, Marcy," said Nora, suddenly appearing from a panel in the ceiling and dropping to the floor. "We have to get out of here."

Nora had a tendency to be blunt, Steve knew. This time, though, he felt that she had taken it too far.

Darcy must have felt the same way, because she turned to Nora and her entire arm began to blaze.

Steve got between Darcy and Nora. "It's okay to feel anger. You can't let it control you, though."

"I'm trying," said Darcy, the flames dying down and then winking out.

Nora said, "This is nice, Steve, you're a great coach and all, but I don't think you heard me. We have to get out. While I was exploring on my own, I saw that the moles were positioning their drill tanks to surround the place. They might wait for us to come out, or they might start them up and turn this place into crumbs."

As soon as she finished speaking, the room started shaking.

That didn't stop Steve's dad from saying, "Nora, when we get back, your mother and I have both agreed that we need to talk to you about running off alone in enemy territory."

A drill tank, sleek and earth-colored, with a massive spinning drill bit on the front of it, came crashing through the ceiling, grinding up everything it touched. The pilot was visible through a glass bubble right above the drill.

It was Drogar.

Another drill tank chewed through the wall behind them. Steve turned so he could keep each drill tank in his sights.

"I have an idea," said Steve. "Nora, do you remember the episode of Kung-Food when Burrito-San needed to infiltrate

Macho Nacho's fortress?"

"Got it," Nora said.

"Okay," Darcy said. "So...?"

Steve grinned. "Use your ghost fire to melt through that cockpit window. We'll be right behind you."

"Wait, what are — ?"

Before Darcy could say anything else, Nora performed the spell of bull strength, picked her up, and threw her like a football. Steve got a running start, Nora laced her fingers together so that her hands formed a little basket, and when Steve planted his foot in her hands, she catapulted him in a wide arc toward the tank.

As Steve sailed through the air, he saw Darcy's hand flare up and watched as the glass cockpit melted like caramel. The mecha-mole pilot had no idea what to do. Darcy looked back and saw Steve flying her way.

"Watch out!" Steve yelled, and Darcy swung herself onto the top of the tank as Steve fell like a meteor toward his target.

Steve's jump kick hit the mecha-mole so hard that it flew out of the pilot's chair and went rolling all the way to the back of the tank. It scurried onto all fours, hit a button on the rear of the tank, and ran out of an emergency exit door.

A moment later, Darcy, Nora, and Steve's parents jumped

into the tank through the melted cockpit bubble.

"Great teamwork," said Steve's mom. "That was perfectly executed."

Steve's dad took control of the tank. "Let's get out of here."

The giant drill on the front of the tank roared to life. With the cockpit broken open like that, there was nothing to quiet the noise.

Darcy got close to Steve. "The next time you're going to have your sister throw me at a tank, promise me you'll do a better job of preparing me."

Steve blushed. "I promise."

The tank angled downward and chewed into the ground. Fine dust began to pour into the cockpit as they went, until Steve's mom performed the spell of windy winds and used it to form a barrier.

"Dad, when did you learn how to pilot one of these?" Steve asked.

"I didn't," he said. "But I wonder what this 'self-destruct' button does."

Steve saw Darcy's eyes get real wide.

"It's a joke," he told her.

"Right," she said. "Of course."

They kept plowing through the ground at a steady rate,

maybe for twenty minutes, when the drill tank punched through a layer of stone and fell into an open cavern.

"We're going down!" said Steve's dad.

Nora and Steve's mom used the spell of windy winds on themselves and everyone in the tank, pinning them all against the ceiling in a cocoon of wind.

The tank landed hard on its side. Steve felt like he was on the world's worst rollercoaster. His stomach was churning and his head was spinning.

Darcy helped him to his feet, and his parents made sure they all got out of the ruined vehicle. Maybe two hundred feet above them, there was a crack in the cavern that must have been along the surface, because beams of moonlight were filtering through.

They heard the approach of another drill tank. He knew, without a doubt, that it was Drogar pursuing them. He would have bet his entire collection of smoke bombs that it would be her. What could they do to get away from her?

Sure enough, the drill tank appeared, though it stopped before it would have plummeted to the ground. The cockpit opened and Drogar got out.

"I would prefer to let my father be the one to get rid of you," she said. "But I guess I'll do it."

She dug down beneath her tank and clawed her way out of a

tunnel so that she arrived right in front of them.

"You can't beat all of us," said Steve's dad.

"Yes I can," said Drogar, blocking as Nora threw a shuriken at her.

There was a low growl from the shadows. Steve glanced over and saw a tall, dark form loping toward them. And another. And another.

"Bear-wolves," said Steve.

It was then that he noticed the cubs hanging back.

"Is that...?" he said.

"Is that what?" said Drogar.

"I think those are the bear-wolf cubs we rescued earlier," he said.

The bear-wolves stepped into the moonlight. Fog began rolling off of them and their giant wolf forms became giant gray-and-black bear forms.

Now they were all larger than Drogar.

Paws the size of basketballs. Claws the size of throwing knives. Teeth the size of...

"Why are some of their teeth so small? They're like kernels of corn," said Steve.

"They're omnivores," said Nora, looking pale. "In bear form, they eat berries *and* meat, so some of their teeth are sharp for tearing, while others don't need to be."

"That's berry interesting," said Steve's dad, "but it's time to get out of here."

The bear-wolf cubs yipped. The adults growled.

They stampeded right past Steve, and they attacked Drogar all at once.

Steve's mom led the way forward, the sounds of the fight fading behind them. The cave passage soon turned completely dark. Steve held his hand in front of his eyes and couldn't even tell that it was there.

"We need light," said Steve's dad.

Darcy's ghost fire danced along her fingertips. It cast deep shadows across everyone's faces. When she looked at Steve, a horrified expression crept across her face.

"It's a spider, isn't it?" asked Steve.

He turned around.

"Boo," said Three.

DARCY

Before Darcy could say anything, Steve's mom was on the offensive. She swung her baseball bat. Three reached up and blocked it with his forearm. He didn't budge.

"Clara," he said, sliding out of the way of her next swing, "why are we doing this?"

"I'm doing this for Vanessa." Steve's mom then performed what Darcy would have called "the spell of the octopus." Her two arms became eight and Darcy had no idea if they were real or merely illusions.

When all of them struck Three at the same time, she got a definitive answer.

Three stumbled right into Ninja Steve's dad, who struck him in the back of the knees with his bat. Three lost his footing, but before he could hit the ground, a puddle of glowing ones and zeroes swallowed him up. When he next appeared, he had a hand on Darcy's back.

"Don't touch me," said Darcy.

"You're all overreacting," he said. "So, in order to make sure we all calm down, I'm going to suggest we all stay very, very still for a little while. I'm here to help you, as long as you are willing to hand me the Nexus key."

"We don't have it," said Darcy. "Drogar destroyed everything in the storage tubes before we could figure out which one was the key."

His grip tightened on Darcy's shoulder, digging into her skin. "That's not true. The vision showed that you all would arrive here with the Nexus key."

"I'm telling the truth," said Darcy. "And I told you not to touch me."

She felt no fear of Three. Having seen Steve's parents actually land attacks on him had shown her that Three wasn't invincible. Right here, right now, they had a chance of defeating him and maybe, finally, getting some answers about what he was doing.

His hand didn't move.

"*You warned him,*" said Toran.

Darcy's entire body radiated with ghost fire. Three's gloved hand burst alight. He flung the glove off before the fire could consume him, too.

The glove hit the cave floor. It bubbled and melted.

Three's exposed hand gave off a dull glow. Darcy recognized it immediately. It was chromega, just like her dagger. There was a difference, however, because Three wiggled his metallic fingers.

"You're a cyborg," said Darcy.

"Maybe," said Three.

Darcy let out a deep breath, and the fire dimmed and flowed back over her body until it was only coating her left hand once again.

"You're in our way, Hiro," said Steve's dad.

"I'm here to help with that," he said. "I'm your quickest way back. Accept my offer and give me the key. I'll have you back in Ninjastoria immediately."

"She told you the truth," said Steve's dad. "We saw Drogar destroy everything. You should open a portal so you can see for yourself."

Three fixed his mask in place with his chromega hand. He crossed his arms.

"Did you investigate your file before you left?" he asked Darcy.

Darcy said nothing.

"Did you find any useful information, like I told you that you would?" he asked.

Steve's mom spoke up. "Don't believe that, Marcy. Everyone from the bureau is going to have interesting info in their files."

She had a point. There was always going to be something mysterious in an agent's files. It was like when people wrote horoscopes: if you provided vague predictions, at least one of them was bound to come true.

"Fine," said Three. "My offer is gone. Best of luck finding your way back."

His watch spilled out glowing numbers and he descended into them. They were left in the tunnel, Darcy's ghost light flickering.

Darcy said, "I keep running into him, but no one will help me figure out what he wants."

There was a silence in the cave.

Steve's mom said, "We have no idea what Hiro really wants. All we know is that after Vanessa went mad from using too many level four spells, he followed her out of Ninjastoria. The next time we saw him, it was years later. He was wearing that mask, using that watch. It's a blend of bureau tech and ninja technique that he created himself. Or maybe Vanessa created it."

Darcy couldn't imagine someone like Three taking orders from anyone, let alone a person who had gone insane. Why would he have followed her?

Steve's dad picked up. "There are several legendary level four spells that dwarf the rest. Our best guess is that Hiro and Vanessa are still seeking them out. Whether or not they intend to use them is beyond the point, because no one is even sure that any of them actually exist."

Darcy looked over at Steve and Nora.

Steve said, "How come nobody has been trying to stop them?"

"We are, constantly," said Steve's mom. "We can't tell you much about the efforts, though, because doing so would endanger the other missions."

"So how are we going to get out of here?" asked Darcy.

Another glowing puddle of ones and zeroes appeared. Three rose up through them.

"I have a new idea," said Three.

STEVE

"You're really annoying," Steve told Three.

Three didn't respond to Steve. Instead, he held up a watch that looked identical to the one his own wrist. He reached out toward Steve and his family.

"This watch has the same portal capabilities as mine, which I'm sure you'll find useful. In fact, the tech is based on what I learned about Ninja Princess Tamika's level four travel scroll. The upside is that it won't corrupt your brain like the spell will," Three said. "It was going to be a gift for Two, but I want to try this, instead."

Steve stared at the watch. Was it possible? Portal travel without a huge risk? He wanted to believe it. Something told him, however, that anything Three gave to anyone was most likely a trap. Still, the thought of being able to go anywhere was a powerful one.

"Nora, I know you're tired of being held back," said Three. "You told me that when I visited your jail cell."

Steve felt a jolt go through his body. He had asked Nora if Three had visited her in jail. Nora said he hadn't.

Nora had lied.

"Stop it, Hiro," said Steve's dad.

"Even now your parents are afraid of you acting

independently," Three said, sliding out of the way as Steve's dad launched an attack on him.

"I know your potential, Nora, because I was like you," he continued, fending off attacks from both of Steve's parents. "The only way for your life to advance is to move forward on your own. You've known this, deep down, for a while."

Three ducked beneath a kick from Steve's mom, blocked a punch from Steve's dad, and casually threw the watch in Nora's direction.

Steve picked up a rock and hurled it. It was a perfect shot, headed straight for the watch.

A throwing knife collided with the rock and knocked it out of the air. Nora had been the one to throw it. She caught the watch and looked it over.

"Nora, put that down!" Steve said. "It's dangerous."

"No," she told him.

Steve knew that something had shifted in Nora. She stared at Steve, her eyes empty. The watch was giving off a dull glow.

Three laughed. It echoed in the cavern. "It works just as easily as you think it does."

Then he was gone again.

"Nora, you can't do this," said Steve. "You belong in Ninjastoria."

"Do I?" she asked. "Weren't you the one who told me that I didn't have any friends? That I've never had a date? I don't belong in Ninjastoria, little brother. So if you want me to stay, you're going to have to take this watch away from me."

Steve felt he had no choice. He launched himself at Nora. He threw his punches as if he was battling a mecha-mole and he did it while his eyes filled with tears. Not once did he land an attack; he couldn't see where he was striking.

Nora dodged every strike, but never struck back.

"Nora, when we get home, we need to have a serious talk," said Steve's mom.

"I'll take us home, but I'm not staying there. The only way I'm ever going to listen to you again is if you defeat me in a fight," said Nora. "And everyone here knows that you don't have a chance of beating me."

Steve realized that his parents had no idea what to do. Nora wasn't a child who could be sent to her room. She had already graduated from college. She had no fear of them.

"You can't trust Three," said Darcy.

"Oh, and I should trust you?" said Nora. "Because, last time I checked, you're a mysterious orphan who just so happened to arrive in our village at the exact same time everything started falling apart."

Nora studied the watch and then pressed a button on the side of it. A purple oval portal made of ones and zeroes opened up beside her. It looked like a stained glass window with sunlight shining through it. When Steve looked, he thought he saw Ninjastoria on the other side.

Nora examined her portal. The thing that she had created. She laughed when she saw it.

"This is unreal," she said, smiling brighter than Steve had ever seen. "I can go wherever I want, whenever I want."

Nora walked through the portal on her own.

Steve's parents ran after her.

He wanted to believe that it was only temporary, that Nora would go back to being his usual older sister in no time. Another part of him, however, felt that something had changed forever.

Steve looked at Darcy and felt horrible. She had just witnessed the worst family argument they'd ever had. Before Arjun's parents had gotten divorced, Steve had seen Arjun's mom and dad get into a nasty argument, and he remembered that all he felt like doing was slinking out the door and running home. He imagined that Darcy was feeling something similar.

"I'm so sorry that you had to see that," said Steve before walking into the portal.

It was nothing more than walking from one place to another.

The portal had transported them into the upper balcony in Swords R Us and Tea B We.

Darcy was right behind him.

"I'm okay, Steve. I'm worried more about you and your family," said Darcy, taking Steve's hands in hers.

"Nora will calm down soon enough," Darcy added, and Steve wasn't sure if she was actually telling the truth or if her spy training was kicking in, helping her to sound convincing.

He saw his parents leaping frantically through the store, calling for Nora. There was no response and she was nowhere to be found.

Then, a pack of brute mecha-moles came tearing through the front doors. A squad of ninjas came chasing after them.

Steve and Darcy let go of each other's hands.

"Let's go," said Darcy.

They leaped over the balcony and landed in the katana aisle. The mecha-moles were caught between them and the other ninjas.

Steve's parents led the charge, baseball bats at the ready. The mecha-moles stood their ground.

Steve's dad did a slide tackle, catching a mecha-mole on the ankle. A ninja from the squad struck from behind with her baseball bat.

One of the brute mecha-moles broke away from the pack and got past Steve's mom. Steve and Darcy got ready to spring out of the way.

There was a *bang* and a cloud of smoke as Steve threw his black smoke bomb right in front of them. In the confusion, he and Darcy were able to get a few feet back.

"That was useless," said one of the mecha-moles, stepping through the cloud of smoke.

"No, it wasn't," said another ninja, who leaped from the top of a nearby shelf and threw her baseball bat at the mecha-mole.

It ducked out of the way, but moved right into the path of another ninja, who delivered a flying elbow strike to its cheek.

"Hi, Steve," said Ninja Kelly, landing next to him.

"Hi," said Steve.

"Oh, great, it's Marcy," said Ninja Steph, landing right in front of her. "Look, Kelly, we showed up just in time. Steve was going to have to do everything by himself if it wasn't for us."

Steve did not like that tone. Steph clearly had no idea what Darcy was capable of.

The mecha-mole grunted. Steve took his baseball bat and went for a swing. The mecha-mole caught the bat and flung Steve into a tower of carefully arranged rubber swords for toddlers. They went everywhere.

The impact knocked the wind out of Steve. His lungs felt like they had collapsed. He kept pulling in air, but his body wasn't responding.

He watched as the mecha-mole knocked Kelly off of her feet with a single kick and then did the same to Steph. Both of the ninja girls had landed near Darcy. Neither one was moving.

That's when Steve felt the ground beneath them start to quake.

DARCY

Darcy felt the earth quaking. She knew exactly what was beneath them. A drill tank.

A small crater started to form. In a few moments, it was likely that the entire floor would drop out from under them.

Darcy looked down at Kelly and Steph, who were both dazed from the mecha-mole's attack. She looked up at the ceiling. If she ran up the side of the shelf and jumped…

Instinct took over. She threw Kelly onto one of her shoulders, Steph onto the other. Darcy clenched her jaw and made her muscles obey. She didn't think about gravity or falling or failure. There was no time for that.

She planted a foot on the shelf and then the other and the next thing she knew, she was running straight up the side of it.

As the floor collapsed and the shelf fell into the pit that opened up, she leaped into the air, twisted, and kicked her feet against the ceiling.

They stuck.

Then, the floor collapsed.

Everything within five aisles was swallowed up by the earth. The entire building shook, and Steph and Kelly both fell from her shoulders.

The girls reached out as they fell.

Kelly grabbed Darcy's left forearm. Steph was clinging to Darcy's right.

Darcy knew that she wouldn't be able to hold on for much longer. She could feel her right heel coming loose from the ceiling.

She saw Steve running toward her. She saw Steve's parents coming from the other direction. But she didn't know if they'd make it in time.

"I'm not letting go!" said Darcy, both to herself and to the girls.

There was a blur of motion and a rush of wind. Someone else had grabbed Ninja Kelly and taken her.

Ninja Gertie.

Darcy reached out and Steph grabbed hold of her other forearm. With a yell, Darcy yanked her up and helped her get her footing on the ceiling.

"I...I...I don't know what to say," said Steph.

Darcy narrowed her eyes.

"You start by saying 'thank you,'" said Gertie. "Didn't anyone teach you proper manners, young lady? When I was your age, if someone saved our lives, we thanked them and then we baked them a double dark chocolate gratitude cake with butter-dream frosting. That's what I would do if I were you."

"Thank you, Marcy," said Ninja Steph, unable to make eye contact. "And...I'm sorry. I'm sorry for everything."

"You're welcome," said Darcy.

They all stood there on the ceiling, looking down at the giant pit that the drill tank had created by tunneling beneath the floor. The mecha-moles had moved elsewhere.

"I always said that this place needed remodeling," said Ninja Gertie. "But I didn't mean it like this."

Darcy nodded. The damage here was unbelievable. She could only imagine what the rest of Ninjastoria looked like.

"Gertie, it's good to see you," said Ninja Steve's mom. "Where is the sisterhood?"

"Nearby. Prince Eldin arrived with a pack of his elite warriors, and they have been battling President Ninja and Sensei Raheem. The sisterhood was on its way to back them up. I broke away to assist here."

"If we can beat Eldin," said Ninja Steve.

"Then maybe we can end this," said Darcy.

STEVE

Steve followed his parents out of Swords R Us. They used a ladder that allowed the workers to access the roof.

Everyone got out and stood beneath the cloudy evening sky. A brisk wind was blowing.

"The mecha-moles are betting that if they can defeat Sensei Raheem and President Ninja in the heart of Ninjastoria, that we will have no choice but to surrender," said Gertie. "We must make our way to the Shrine of the First Ninja."

Of course. The Shrine of the First Ninja. They would challenge the ninjas at the very center of their village, the place where the First Ninja had declared the creation of Ninjastoria.

They ran to the edge of the roof and leaped off. The Shrine of the First Ninja was not far from here.

Steve's legs were killing him and he bet that everyone was feeling exhausted. His stomach was growling.

"You need to eat!" said Ninja Gertie. Out of nowhere, she flung homemade energy bars to everyone. "These are mellow-berry crunch bars, freshly baked this morning."

"Weren't you fighting with mecha-moles this morning?" asked Steve.

"Yes, but Morris and I still decided to bake our crunch bars like we do every weekend," said Gertie. "We can't let the mecha-moles take that from us."

Steve eagerly devoured the food. Mellowberries were golden orange, slightly sweet, and only grew in Ninjastoria. Gertie had mixed them with crispy rice puffs and a salty peanut-butter swirl. It was perfect.

The battle had left no part of Ninjastoria untouched. Storefronts were scuffed up, windows were cracked, and several buildings had collapsed.

"We're going to have to rebuild so much," said Steve.

"We'll do what we have to do," said his mom.

The sound of battle loomed ahead. Crashing. Thumping. Clanking. Roaring.

Steve could see the Shrine of the First Ninja. It was a series of black stone pillars that formed a wide circle, wide enough that it took nearly a half-hour to walk the full circle. In the center of it, there would be a katana with a white handle. Half of its blade was sunk into a metal cube and fused together.

The shrine was swarming with ninjas on one side and mecha-moles attacking from the other.

Steve looked up at the rooftop of the Museum of Sharp Objects, which was the closest building to the shrine.

"They're about to launch the cat-a-pults," he said.

"Why did you say it with pauses between the syllables?"

Darcy asked him.

"That's the only way to say it. Cat. Pause. Uh. Pause. Pult."

"But you're supposed to say it all together: catapult."

"Oh," said Steve. "You are thinking of a different device. This is a cat-a-pult."

Steve pointed to one that was about to be loaded up. A ninja wound a crank that pulled back an oversized wooden spoon. A cluster of ninja cats climbed in. Then, the ninja pulled a lever and the cats were flung in a smooth arc toward their targets. Darcy frowned as she watched five cats go sailing into battle.

"Isn't that dangerous for the cats?" Darcy asked. "Isn't that animal cruelty?"

Steve laughed. "The cats were the ones who came up with the design and asked us to help them build them. Besides, cats always land on their feet. Unless there's an enemy nearby. Then, a cat will always land on its enemy."

Ninja Gertie piped up. "It's scientific fact. Alberta Meinstein was the one who tested the initial hypothesis, and her experiments were repeated by other scientists until we could confirm it as a theory."

And then there was no more time for talking. There were waves of mecha-moles and drill tanks advancing on the shrine or drilling up through the ground around it.

Steve saw some of the other members of the Sisterhood of Butt-Kicking. He tried to stay with his parents, but a drill tank fired a drill missile, and everyone had to scatter.

The scout mecha-moles in this wave were all carrying pairs of metal mallets, joined together by a chain. Some of them had large batteries strapped to their backs, supplying extra power to their claws. Steve readied his baseball bat. Darcy gripped her dagger in one hand and set her other hand aflame.

A pack of ninja cats rained down from the sky. The black felines all landed on scouts and dug their claws in. Some of the moles shrieked, others flailed around, trying to shake the cats off.

In front of Steve, a drill tank came to the surface. Three brute mecha-moles climbed out to fight. They all set their sights on Steve.

Three cats formed a defensive line in front of him.

Then, Sensei Chow arrived.

He held one of his heavy spatulas in one hand and a pot lid in the other. Strapped across his back was some kind of squirt gun.

"Ninja Steve, it's time for them to get *served*."

Steve thought it was a terrible line.

The cats hissed, and all three of them attacked the same brute mecha-mole. One landed on its leg, one on the shoulder, and one on the back of its neck. They started scratching.

Sensei Chow performed the spell of the vampire hunter. Ten cloves of garlic appeared in his hand. He smashed them with the spatula against his palm and handed the fragrant garlic paste to Ninja Steve, who wasn't exactly thrilled to be receiving it.

"Their noses are extra-sensitive," said Sensei Chow. "You know what to do."

Steve wished that he still had a Mega Fart Bomb XL or two. The garlic paste would have to do, instead.

The mecha-mole that Steve attacked was huge, yes, but Steve trusted his own speed. The mecha-mole swiped at him, and Steve slipped alongside it. He jumped up and smashed all of the garlic paste straight into the brute mecha-mole's nose.

It yelled, thrashed, started coughing, and then collapsed in tears.

The ninja glider squads began their assault, flying overhead and dropping down into the middle of the enemy ranks. Steve also caught sight of Ninjastoria's two rival soccer clubs kicking soccer balls into clusters of mecha-mole soldiers.

The cats were still keeping one of the moles busy until Sensei Chow told them to move. Sensei Chow readied the squirt gun. He pulled the trigger.

"Anchovy paste cannon!" he yelled, and blasted the two

mecha-moles. The smell of the anchovy paste was so potent that it made Steve's eyes water even from a distance.

But that had only taken care of three of them.

There was still an entire army.

A thousand more mecha-moles were charging from the same side, forming a giant wall, driving the ninjas back toward the heart of the shrine. Thousands more could be seen tunneling up through the dirt.

Steve began to wonder if today was the day that Ninjastoria would fall.

DARCY

Darcy knew that now was not the time to hold anything back. Her ghost fire—her curse—was a strength that no one else in Ninjastoria possessed.

Instead of hiding it, she let her left hand blaze.

Two scouts lunged for her. She touched her flaming hand to their metal claws in quick succession and watched as the metal part melted away, leaving only their natural claws. Unarmed, they ran away.

"Well done," said Toran.

Despite her little victory, she was starting to doubt that the ninjas would be able to pull this one off. They were using everything they could against the moles: blasts of lightning and ice, tornadoes, rumble-bees. No matter what they did, the moles kept coming.

A fresh battalion of at least fifty brute mecha-moles dug themselves out of the ground. Each one carried a drill lance: a six-foot spear with a rotating drill tip at the end.

Evelyn had taught her about dealing with long-range weapons. The very first piece of advice was to avoid them entirely. If you had to engage, the first step was closing the distance between yourself and your foe.

"Sisterhood, let's get in formation!" came a shout.

Ninja Amari landed on top of one of the black pillars. She rested her sledgehammer on one shoulder.

At the base of the pillar, the entire Sisterhood of Butt-Kicking gathered and faced east. They held baseball bats and hockey sticks and bo staffs and nunchakus.

"Ninja Marcy! We're waiting for you!" Amari called.

Darcy smirked. She found a spot between Ninja Gertie and Ninja Steve's mom.

Darcy didn't see the motions that Amari performed, but she definitely saw the ball of lightning that spiraled down from above and scattered the lancers.

"CHARGE!" shouted Amari.

The sisterhood surged toward the wall of enemies with the force of a tsunami.

A lancer thrust its spear at Gertie, who leaped onto it like it was a balance beam. With one kick, she broke the lance in half and then jumped away. Darcy threw all of her weight into a jumping elbow strike that caught the mecha-mole on its chin and knocked it flat on its back.

She drew her chromega dagger and began cutting straight through the lances, allowing the other members of the sisterhood to fight the unarmed moles.

All around them, the sisterhood worked as a team, sweeping

the enemy back and back and back, pressing them away from the Shrine of the First Ninja.

They were breaking the moles' advances.

They had given Ninjastoria a fighting chance.

STEVE

He heard Ninja Amari direct the Sisterhood of Butt-Kicking to turn their attention to the wall of mecha-moles closing in from the east. The rest of the ninja forces followed behind them.

Steve saw that his dad was headed to the front lines of the battle. Steve went after him.

At the very center of the front lines, Prince Eldin and his elite guard squad of brute mecha-moles were in a furious battle with Sensei Raheem, President Ninja, and Steve's mom.

Sensei Raheem was bruised on his face and his arms, defeated mecha-moles flying away from him in every direction. He performed the spell of the ferocious hedgehog, a defensive maneuver that turned his mohawk into actual spikes on his head and kept enemies from jumping on him. He was battling four mecha-moles that wore golden armor that had drill bits on nearly every limb.

Steve saw his mother fending off three more moles by herself until Steve's dad arrived.

President Ninja was using his famous electric-eel style of battle, which mimicked the slick and sudden movements of the infamous sea creature. Prince Eldin, in his black and gold armor, had a tough time landing a strike.

Steve knew that the electric-eel style was defensive, made to wear an opponent out. From the looks of it, though, President Ninja was the one who was worn out.

Sensei Raheem unleashed the spell of ten thousand crying babies, which caused everyone to clamp their hands over their ears. With a single spin-kick, the legendary hero of Ninjastoria knocked out all of his opponents.

President Ninja, who had been caught off guard by Sensei Raheem's technique, stumbled, and Prince Eldin managed to punch him right on the nose.

Without a second thought, Ninja Steve launched himself at Prince Eldin. He readied his baseball bat and swung.

He missed.

The prince ducked beneath it, yanked the bat out of Steve's hands, and then swept Steve's feet out from under him. Steve flopped on the ground like a fish out of water...or a winged armadillo *in* the water.

"Elom!" yelled Prince Eldin. "Get over here!"

Sensei Raheem and both of Steve's parents joined in the assault against Eldin, throwing a storm of strikes that looked like a blur.

The young prince poked his head out from behind one of the black columns of the shrine. He had been hiding there, avoiding the battle.

"Your son isn't a warrior," said Steve. "He doesn't want to fight me and I don't want to fight him."

Elom adjusted his helmet. "I'm not a coward."

He approached Steve and flexed his claws. Steve stayed light on his feet, hopping back and forth. Elom slashed, and Steve caught him by the wrist.

"I don't want to become a slave!" shouted Elom.

"We don't have slaves here," said Steve. "We never have. Slavery is the worst."

That seemed to stun the prince. His arms went slack.

"What do you mean? Dad told me that Ninjastoria had more slaves than any other country. Are you calling my dad a liar?"

"We don't have slaves. We don't cook other ninjas and eat them. We don't have holidays where we dress prisoners up like mecha-moles and hit them with drumsticks," said Steve. "Not a single thing you've said to me about my people is true."

"All ninjas are liars," he growled. "You're trying to get me to lower my guard and it almost worked, you lying ninja peasant!"

Elom punched Steve in the face. The punch barely hurt. It was probably the weakest punch Steve had encountered in years. He knew, though, that the only way this could end would be if he delivered a sound trouncing to Prince Elom. Of course, Steve didn't want to actually hurt him. He was the least threatening mecha-mole of them all.

Steve drove a half-strength palm strike into Elom's armored chest plate. He had to try really hard to make it a weak strike. The young mole screamed and collapsed. Steve knew that Elom was pretending to be unconscious and he was okay with that.

Prince Eldin was still trying to fend off Sensei Raheem, President Ninja, and Steve's parents when Steve called out to him, "Your son was no match for me, Prince Eldin."

"My son, then, has failed his royal heritage," Eldin said. "In order to restore honor to the throne, I will have to take care of all of you."

He threw Steve's mom to the ground, punched Steve's dad out of the way, barreled into President Ninja, and made a beeline for Steve.

Steve knew that if he wanted to use the spell of melted time, this was the moment.

He didn't get the chance.

Sensei Raheem shoved Steve out of the way, but it left Raheem with no time to block Eldin's jump-kick.

The prince's massive foot collided with Raheem's face, and Steve watched, horrified, as Ninjastoria's greatest living hero was knocked out.

DARCY

Darcy had been a part of the sisterhood's charge and felt her spirits lift as the other ninjas fed on their momentum.

But then, drill tanks began to arrive on the *other* side of the shrine. The majority of the ninja forces were busy fighting in the opposite direction.

As more and more drill tanks broke through the surface, the mecha-moles gave a cheer. The ninjas were surrounded, caught between two walls of mecha-mole forces that threatened to crush them in the middle.

Darcy watched as Drogar, encased in her full battle armor, stood atop one of the tanks. The bear-wolves may have attacked her, but they hadn't stopped her for good.

Even though none of the ninjas could hear what Drogar said to her troops, it didn't matter. Her return to the battlefield had given the moles new energy. They regrouped; they got into neat lines. Those who still had weapons were up front.

Darcy saw the concern on Ninja Amari's face. She saw Gertie looking absolutely exhausted. She watched as the ninjas regrouped and split their forces to face their enemies on either side.

Darcy knew that her dagger could cut through some of the tanks. She knew that her ghost fire could melt down parts of the tanks, too. Both options, however, meant having to get incredibly close. Much too close for comfort.

The cat-a-pults were reloaded. The glider squads took to the air once more. The soccer teams unloaded one final bag of soccer balls. Sensei Chow readied his battle spatulas.

Darcy knew that this was going to be their last stand.

STEVE

Steve saw Sensei Raheem get hit with the full force of Prince Eldin's jump-kick. He watched his teacher fall to the ground, unconscious. A terrible guilt welled up inside of Steve. This was all his fault.

Eldin spared no time in striking Steve. The mole prince's fists were almost too fast to see, and the impact dropped Steve flat on his back.

Prince Eldin laughed and pointed at President Ninja.

"Raheem has been defeated. Your delinquent trickster is down after a single rush from me. You are caught between my ground forces and my sister's tank squadron. You should surrender, President Ninja. Say, 'We surrender.'"

The battlefield grew quiet as all eyes turned to Eldin and President Ninja.

President Ninja straightened his moustache.

"Prince Eldin, you would like me to say *two* very specific words, wouldn't you?" asked President Ninja. "*Two words* that would be of incredible significance?"

"Yes, President Ninja. Say 'We surrender' and that will be the end of it," said Eldin.

Steve watched the president thoughtfully twirl his moustache.

"Then perhaps the people of Ninjastoria should say the *two words* with me. They should join me as we say *two words* that will affect all of Ninjastoria and the history of our village. *Two words* that I will be forever known for saying."

Steve smiled. Prince Eldin had no idea what was coming next, but Steve and all of Ninjastoria's warriors were ready.

President Ninja shouted, "Prince Eldin, the people of Ninjastoria would like to say two very important words to you, so that you know that all of us truly mean it. Ninjas! On the count of four: one, two, three, four!"

At once, in unison, all of the ninjas on the battlefield screamed at the top of their lungs, "SHUT UP!"

And they began the fight once more, despite the odds and despite the exhaustion.

Steve saw Darcy and the sisterhood were nearby, turning their energies back toward Drogar's tanks. Darcy's ghost fire was blazing and Steve was glad to see that she wasn't hiding it anymore. She could do amazing things, and even though her talents were different from everyone else's, it was something that made her valuable.

Steve's parents landed beside him.

"We should help the rest of the sisterhood," Steve said.

"Fine, just stay with us, Steve," said his dad.

The tanks fired off a series of drill bullets that scattered the ninja forces

Steve and his parents wound up with Darcy and Gertie. They tried another charge and were once again driven back by the tanks' superior firepower.

Steve's parents and Gertie all performed the spell of dragon breath, which was enough to melt down the front of one of the tanks. Another tank immediately took its place.

"Mom and Dad," said Steve. "Are we going to lose?"

DARCY

"Things are not looking good," said Steve's dad, and Darcy knew it was the truth.

"We've all shown incredible toughness," said his mom. "I'm afraid it hasn't been enough, though. We need to prepare to retreat and see if we can find another way to continue the fight."

The moles had defeated the bureau, and they were going to conquer Ninjastoria, too. Months ago, if someone had told Darcy that all of this was going to happen, she never would have believed it.

"I wish the samurai were here," said Ninja Steve.

Gertie looked at him and snorted. "If wishes were armor, we'd *all* be samurai."

Darcy had never heard that phrase before. It made sense, though.

"No, I'm not talking about having armor," said Steve. "Their earth-shake magic. The moles have an advantage because they can tunnel and dig. Our border wall didn't do anything to keep them out. The samurai could have detected their tunneling, though."

"Border walls are always bad at keeping people out," said Gertie. "I remember when that idiot leader of ours first proposed building the thing—not President Ninja, mind you. One that came way before him. He was the worst."

Darcy couldn't focus on what they were saying. She could only focus on the mecha-moles, whose forces looked even bigger and stronger than before.

Then, up in the sky, she saw something.

It looked like…it looked like…a group of flying armadillos?

STEVE

"Yes!" shouted Steve, as he spied the reinforcements in the sky. "They're here."

He could barely contain his energy.

From the sky, a thousand samurai descended on their flying armadillos. Although the gray, winged armadillos were naturally armored, each animal wore a battle helmet.

At the head of the charge, wearing silver armor striped red, blue, and green, was Four-Star General Aaliyah Nakashima.

General Nakashima stood up on the back of her armadillo and drew two wooden swords. Steve watched in awe as she did a swan dive off of the armadillo. The battle beast curled itself into a ball. Hundreds of curled-up armadillos fell like cannon-balls on the mecha-moles' drill tanks, destroying them.

Half of the samurai forces struck in the middle of Drogar's gathered battalion, putting their earth-shake magic to use. The ground rumbled and rolled. The tunnels that the moles had used to swarm into Ninjastoria were being closed.

Steve was watching his homeland get healed right before his eyes.

Ninja Amari was helping Sensei Raheem walk away from battle while Sensei Chow fought off any mecha-moles who tried to take a cheap shot at the injured Raheem.

Even with the samurai forces, there was still one huge problem remaining. Prince Eldin was not going to pack up and leave.

Steve watched as his parents, Ninja Gertie, and President Ninja all squared-off against Eldin once more.

He turned to Darcy. "I think I know how we can end this."

DARCY

When Steve told her his plan, she knew it was a good one. While she didn't love the idea of Steve acting evil, she knew that the end result would play out perfectly. Well, there were two possible end results, although she was ninety-nine percent sure she knew which scenario was going to unfold.

She watched as Steve approached the spot where Prince Elom still lay, pretending to be unconscious. Darcy found it remarkable that he was committed to staying still until the battle was over.

Then, Steve yanked the prince to his feet and put him in a full nelson.

"Ouch!" said Prince Elom. "Let go of me, ninja, before the infectious bacteria in your breath gives me a disease."

Darcy stood by as Steve got Eldin's attention. "Prince Eldin, I have taken your son as a hostage!"

Then, Steve did his best impersonation of a villain's laugh. It was loud and it was terrible. Ninja Steve was not a great actor.

"If you want your son back, unharmed, you will order your forces to leave Ninjastoria," Steve said.

Darcy got ready. This was the part where Eldin would attack Steve in order to save his son. Darcy would get between them and use her ghost fire to melt his armor. Then, hopefully, the other ninjas would join in to defeat Eldin.

Eldin smiled. "Keep him. He will break free of any prison you put him in."

Steve's blank stare let Darcy know that he hadn't been expecting that, either. There would be no charge to rescue Elom. Which meant...

Darcy closed the distance between herself and Eldin. She unleashed her ghost fire. She aimed her palm strike at Eldin's chest plate.

He sidestepped with incredible speed, grabbed Darcy by the elbow, and threw her into the air.

As Darcy hurtled away, she watched as Ninja Steve's parents managed to sling Ninja Gertie into the sky, on a collision course with Darcy.

Gertie held out her palms and said, "Marcy, pretend my palms are the ceiling."

Darcy flipped so that her feet were pointed toward Gertie. When her heels touched Gertie's palms, they stuck there for an instant, a perfect lock.

"Go get him, girl," said Gertie. "Burn bright."

Darcy thought back to Ninja Gertie telling her to be proud of the things that made her strong. Yes, she had tiger stripes on her upper arm. Yes, her ability stemmed from a curse. None of that mattered. The ninjas wielded the elements through their techniques. This was *her* technique.

Darcy launched off of Gertie's palms and shot back down toward Eldin, who had his hands full fighting President Ninja and Sensei Chow.

Fire coated her left hand. She hit Prince Eldin's armor on his left shoulder pad, which immediately erupted in flames. With a yell, he unhinged all of the armor on his upper body and flung it away.

That moment was all they needed.

President Ninja threw a jumping, spinning back-kick that blasted Prince Eldin across the battlefield. He crashed into the cockpit of Drogar's drill tank.

Sensei Raheem, still a little unsteady, used a technique that made an ordinary tomato become twenty times the size of a drill tank. With the help of Ninja Amari, Sensei Chow, and Steve's parents, they hurled the gargantuan tomato right onto Eldin and Drogar. It totally flattened their tank and left half of the mecha-mole army covered in tomato pulp.

The ninjas had seized the upper hand.

The moles began to retreat.

STEVE

Steve was left holding onto Prince Elom. While the young prince had been trying to break free at first, he gave up the moment his father left him as a hostage.

There was no need to keep Elom in a full nelson anymore. The mecha-mole had gone completely slack and sank to his knees. He started crying.

"My father abandoned me," said Elom.

He had. Steve was sure that Eldin believed in his son's ability to escape from Ninjastoria, which told Steve that Prince Eldin refused to see the truth about his own son. Elom was not going to be a great fighter. He wasn't going to be a great military commander like his father, either.

"Your dad thinks you're strong, Elom," said Steve. "He didn't leave you to be mean to you. He thinks you'll be able to find a way out on your own."

The prince sniffled. "I won't, though. Everyone knows that ninja prison is the worst place you can end up. They feed you glue for breakfast, the prison mattress is stuffed full of cactus needles, and the floors are all blocks of ice."

That was a very creative approach to prison. Steve was glad that none of the ninjas had ever thought to do those things.

"Elom, I went to prison once. It's nothing at all like that," said

Steve. "Ninjas are mostly very nice people."

Elom didn't hear or pretended not to hear. A squad of ninjas came over and carried him away. Steve wondered if anything would ever change Elom's mind or if he would forever feel like ninjas were lying, abusive creatures. He had little doubt that the mole prince would be scared and alone, despite whatever outward appearance he tried to put on.

Steve's parents came by.

"We're proud of you, Steve," said his mom. "You've acted like a true ninja."

"Are you ready to go home?" asked his dad.

He wasn't sure what kind of homecoming it would be. What if the house had been damaged by the moles? Or, even worse, what if it had been completely destroyed?

"We might have some maintenance work to do," said his mom, her thoughts in line with his.

"Nora and I can help," said Steve, finishing the sentence before he remembered the truth.

His dad's eyes teared up. His mother looked down. Steve wished that he could tunnel away like the moles.

"I'm sorry," said Steve. "I didn't mean to…"

His dad hugged him. "It's okay, Steve. We'll get her to come home."

Steve nodded.

They'd find a way.

They had to.

DARCY

She saw Steve and his parents coming her way. They looked so tired and she knew that she must have looked the same.

"Marcy, you might be the toughest ninja we've got," said Ninja Steve's mom.

"Careful with the compliments," said Gertie. "If she hears too many of them, she'll get carried away and then she won't train as hard."

"Fine," said Steve's mom. "Marcy, once we've got Ninjastoria in a better state, you'll be hearing from Ninja Amari. The Sisterhood of Butt-Kicking is going to hold an induction ceremony. I'll be recommending you as a new recruit."

Darcy stood a little taller. If they were willing to have her, she would definitely join.

Steve's parents backed away for a moment to speak quietly about something else, which left Darcy and Steve together.

"You had a great plan," said Darcy.

"You had cool moves," said Steve. "It's hard to believe that you haven't always been a ninja."

Darcy thought about what her life could be like if she stayed in Ninjastoria. She could learn more techniques. She could train with the Sisterhood of Butt-Kicking. She could make new friends.

"So, Steve, I think that we're going to have to postpone our ice cream run for a little while," she told him. "But once everything's open again, we should totally go."

"You got it," said Steve.

She gave him a hug and waved goodbye as he left with his parents.

As they walked away, Darcy wondered what it would be like in their house tonight without Nora. She knew that Steve's family was not going to have an easy road ahead of them, not until they found her and brought her home.

Darcy wondered about her old home. Now that the moles had been driven out of Ninjastoria, would they also abandon the bureau headquarters?

Before she could think too much about it, Gertie flagged her down.

"Tonight, Marcy, we are going to cook up a storm," she said. "Biscuits, jalapeño mashed potatoes, spicy chicken, and a six-layer pudding for dessert. I'm going to call it, 'The Marcy Victory Special.' How's that for a name?"

"I approve," said Darcy.

Later that evening, as she sat at the dinner table with Gertie and Morris, Darcy considered her good fortune.

"The past is gone and this is your life now," she thought.

And, for the first time, that thought brought a smile to her face.

STEVE

The first week that followed the war was not easy, despite the fact that their house was left almost completely untouched by the moles. That made Steve's street one of the lucky ones.

Many of the ninjas closer to the center of Ninjastoria had lost their homes entirely. President Ninja and the Sisterhood of Butt-Kicking were busy converting the school and the university into temporary housing for the ninjas who needed a place to live.

Although Ninjastoria had driven the mecha-moles out, it had left Steve shaken up. If Ninjastoria couldn't defend itself without the help of others, then he didn't feel safe.

He was sitting on the ceiling in the living room and he was venting his frustrations to his parents. "We have all of these techniques and all of this training. How come it wasn't enough?"

His mother and father didn't seem to have a good answer for him.

"And another thing," Steve said. "We have ultra-powerful level four techniques and *no one is allowed to use them*. Couldn't a few of them have turned the tide of the war? Isn't there some kind of technique that can blow up The Mole Republic?"

This time, they had an answer.

"Yes, Steve, there was a spell like that," said his mother. "A spell that could destroy an entire country. The ninja who created it never told anyone how to do it. She never wrote it down on a scroll. She knew it was far too powerful and that one day the wrong ninja would use it and it would be a disaster for our entire world. We are very thankful that it doesn't exist. One day, I hope you will be, too."

Steve couldn't perform the spell of dragon breath, but he felt like he was about to breathe fire, anyway. "That's so *dumb*! It could have prevented this entire war. Then, I'd be back in Sensei Raheem's class, Nora would still be here, and Samurai Sam wouldn't have left."

Suddenly, the fire Steve felt was turning into tears. He couldn't hold them back. Steve jumped down from the ceiling and ran to his room. He paced up and down the walls.

After ten minutes of fruitless pacing, he called Samurai Sam. No answer. Yesterday, they had spent an hour talking about everything that had happened. Even with the war being over, Sam said his family wouldn't be coming back to Ninjastoria for at least another month.

When he was sure that his parents weren't going to come after him, he cracked open his door and then silently made his way to his sister's room. He turned the knob and walked inside. Everything was exactly as it always was: swords on display, shuriken pouches at the ready, Shinobi-Onsay poster on the wall. Perfectly arranged and perfectly empty.

"Why did you do this, Nora?" he asked.

He was about to leave her room when he heard his parents talking about Nora.

"President Ninja has plenty of people looking for her," said his mom. "They'll find her and she'll come back to us."

"What if she's out there with Hiro, trying to find a Nexus key?" his dad asked. "What if they open it?"

That sounded like something Nora would do. It was a challenge beyond anything anyone had ever presented her. He didn't want to believe it, though.

"I doubt it. If anything, I think we'll see her turn up at the Unlimited Power Tournament," said Steve's mom. "Hiro talked about finding her a teacher, right? The tournament would be a chance for her to prove her skills."

"The tournament isn't for another six months," said Steve's dad, and then he started to cry.

Steve felt his own heart sink way down. He retreated back to his room, found Sensei Raheem's book, and opened it up to the table of contents. Chapter twenty-five was entitled, "How to Enter and Win the Unlimited Power Tournament."

If there was even a chance that Nora was going to be there, then Steve wanted to make sure he had a reason to be there, too.

DARCY

Two weeks after the end of the war, Gertie was teaching Darcy the art of moving meditation. Darcy enjoyed being in the training room for a peaceful lesson, because normally her time spent in that room made her sweat and get hurt.

For the past hour, they had been doing their moving meditation while on the ceiling. Whatever magic Ninjastoria seemed to have, it had finally found its way to her. Now she could stand on walls and ceilings whenever she wanted. That meant it was only a matter of time before she could start working with more powerful techniques.

When their meditation wrapped up, it meant that there would be thirty minutes until the next lesson began. Darcy always used this time to ask Gertie lots of questions about ninja life.

"I've been curious about how techniques work," Darcy said to Gertie. "Can't any kid just follow the steps and be able to cast the same powerful spell as an adult ninja?"

Gertie took a seat on the ceiling, closed her eyes, and slowly opened them. "While most of us start out very weak, our techniques get stronger over time. If you and I both used the spell of angry rumble-bees, I would summon more bees."

"And what's the cost?"

"Most adult ninjas can only manage about six techniques per

day. It's like this well of power that's inside of you and sleeping is what replenishes it. Some of us, however, have more power than others. Ninja Gretel was said to be able to do over fifty. She even invented a famous technique that would get you out of the woods if you were lost. Sadly, the steps to performing that one were forgotten over time."

Gertie signaled that it was time to leave the ceiling. She and Darcy bowed to each other.

"Enjoy your afternoon, Marcy," said Gertie, and she left.

Darcy had an hour until she was meeting Ninja Steve. They couldn't go to Fro-Zen, because it had been damaged in the war and was being rebuilt. Instead, they were getting drinks and snacks at Throwing Star Buck's.

She stood in her room in Gertie and Morris's basement, looking through her closet. They had taken her out to get her more ninja-styled clothes and accessories, including a black flower crown that many of the ninja girls around town were wearing. Following the war, the lead singer of Kaiju and the Battle Rangers had worn a black flower crown at the victory celebration concert.

Darcy had overheard a group of younger ninja girls saying that Kaiju was the new Shinobi-Onsay.

She looked at herself in the mirror that hung in her closet and she put on the flower crown. It made her happy, even though she knew it was just a decoration that lots of other girls had. She wondered if Steve would like it.

All of Ninjastoria was focused on rebuilding. Darcy passed by Kickin' Cake, where a crew of ninjas was repairing the roof and putting in a new display window. The movie theater, which had been busted up by a drill missile, was being surveyed by the reconstruction team.

The businesses that had made it through unharmed were opening late and closing early so that more people could pitch in and help out in other places. School was cancelled for a full eight weeks. The teachers were organizing the students into groups that would distribute supplies or assist in construction projects. Darcy was in a group with Ninja Arjun and Ninja Kelly. Ever since Darcy had saved Kelly from falling in Swords R Us, she had been much more pleasant. In fact, she had stopped hanging out with Ninja Steph entirely.

Darcy was a block away from Throwing Star Buck's, thinking about getting a green tea latte.

"There's something I've been thinking about," said Toran, and Darcy jumped.

"Did you have to scare me like that?" Darcy asked in her head.

Toran ignored her question. *"It was said that the samurai had a spiritual master who lived at the bottom of the ocean. She mastered the sword to the point where it bored her. She began to develop what she called 'the blade of the mind' and aimed to hone her magical prowess until she could use it like a sword."*

"I don't like where this is going," Darcy thought.

Toran went on. *"Three thousand years ago, Bushido Gardens was invaded by Darkwalkers. They are ghosts of a — "*

Darcy had heard enough. *"I know what Darkwalkers are. They're from a book series. They look like humans, but they turn into dark silhouettes at night, and possess people. They're monsters, Toran. Well, except for Allison, because — "*

"I assure you, Darkwalkers are very real," said Toran. *"But that is not the point of telling you this story."*

"Why, then?"

"The samurai's blade of the mind was able to cut the Darkwalkers away from those who were possessed. Without her, Bushido Gardens would have fallen. There was a small group of samurai who stuck with her after that and learned her art."

Darcy saw exactly where Toran was headed. *"You think that if we go to Bushido Gardens, we might be able to find a samurai who can separate us."*

"Exactly."

"Why would I want to set you loose?" asked Darcy. *"I know that the ninjas sealed you away for a reason."*

"Yes, they did," said Toran. *"They were clever about it, too. They waited until my battle with the other ghosts crossed over into Ninjastoria. It wasn't really about saving Ninjastoria, though."*

"What was it about, then?"

"President Ninja wanted me sealed away for a very different reason. He somehow figured out that I could track down the Nexus keys," said Toran.

Upon hearing "Nexus keys," Darcy immediately thought of her parents.

Toran continued, *"If we can get the samurai to set me free, I will help you find the Nexus keys, Darcy."*

She shivered. *"You'll run off the moment you're free. Or you'll destroy me. Or you'll set out to free the other captured ghosts. Why would I ever trust you on this?"*

"Because," Toran said, *"there's something in the Nexus that I want, too. And it requires the help of a human to get it."*

THE END

NOTE FROM THE AUTHOR:

Thank you for reading Mecha-Mole Mayhem! I hope you had fun joining Darcy and Steve in their latest adventure.

I'd like to ask you for a small favor. **Can you please post a review of this book on Amazon and Goodreads?** Even if it's one or two sentences, every Amazon review that gets posted helps more readers discover Agent Darcy and Ninja Steve.

And, finally, my fans are my favorite people, and I love hearing from them. You can always contact me through my website, and while you're there, you can check out the latest blog posts or sign up for the Ninja Newsletter to get special updates on Agent Darcy and Ninja Steve.

ACKNOWLEDGMENTS

Where to begin?

Thank you to all of my beta readers. You saw this book before it was this book and gave me all kinds of new ideas to consider.

My editor, Shannon A. Thompson, knocked it out of the park on this one. I felt like the draft I sent to her was — to use teacher terms here — an 85%. Her insight, suggestions, and willingness to challenge my writing skills have transformed this novel into something I am 100% proud to present to you.

Cover artist master, Tristan George, has delivered yet another five-star portrayal of Darcy and Steve. He's also offered up the very first glimpse of Ninjastoria and I love it.

I'm looking forward to bringing the team back together when book four takes shape. See you then!

BONUS CONTENT: ARTICLE

Cartoons Make You a Better Writer by Grant Goodman (Originally Published on Shannon A. Thompson's Blog)

When I sat down to write the first *Agent Darcy & Ninja Steve* novel, what really drove me was my love of cartoons. I wanted to create — in written form — the cartoon series I always wanted to see.

I grew up with the original *Teenage Mutant Ninja Turtles*. I was glued to the sofa when they stormed the Technodrome to fight Shredder or when they teamed up with Casey Jones. Each episode had cool fight scenes, a sci-fi invention, and at least one funny line from Michelangelo. The turtles were my first obsession and they propelled me to join a martial arts school when I was in elementary school.

My elementary school mornings and weekends were filled with *Tom and Jerry Kids*, *Inspector Gadget*, *X-Men*, *Spiderman*, and *Batman: The Animated Series*. While most of them were in short story format, the *X-Men*, *Spiderman*, and *Batman* series began to introduce me to the idea that 30 minute cartoons could build a larger story. *Spiderman* had "The Alien Costume" arc, which gave Venom's origin story over the course of three episodes. But that wasn't quite enough. I wanted a longer storyline.

The first episode of *Dragonball Z* aired when I was in 6th grade and when I saw it, my head nearly exploded. A series in which nearly every episode built off of the last. A cast of characters who did martial arts AND threw fireballs. An entire universe of heroes and villains, legends and lore.

DBZ led me into the wide, wild catalog of Japanese animation that revealed an entire cultural art form that offered a great deal of respect to storytelling in animated form.

All of it — every episode of every series I ever watched — has somehow contributed to my abilities as a writer, and it will for you, too. You learn how to plot an action scene that matters, because you see plenty of them that don't. You learn how to keep two characters pining for each other in order to build tension between them. You learn the importance of a cliffhanger to keep your audience hooked.

Most importantly, however, watching cartoons will teach you how to keep your imagination active, because without a strong imagination, you're going to write something boring.

If you're aspiring to write a MG or YA sci-fi/fantasy action series, my best advice to you is to watch cartoons. Lots of them. Go watch the first season of *The Legend of Korra* for a masterclass in serious-but-not-pitch-black YA storytelling. Seek out *Samurai Jack* for how to do fight scenes that flow.

This may be the only time anyone in your life tells you this: stop reading for a bit and start watching!

ABOUT THE AUTHOR

Grant Goodman teaches English classes
in Montgomery County, Maryland.

He is fueled by *Over the Garden Wall*, homemade chicken
broth, and the *Sushi Go Party!* card game.

You can follow him on Instagram: @grantgoodmanauthor

Made in the USA
Middletown, DE
18 September 2019